More Than a Friend

More Than a Friend

Chad Taylor

Writers Club Press
New York San Jose Lincoln Shanghai

More Than a Friend

All Rights Reserved © 2000 by Chad Taylor

No part of this book may be reproduced or transmitted in any form or by any means, graphic, electronic, or mechanical, including photocopying, recording, taping, or by any information storage retrieval system, without the permission in writing from the publisher.

Writers Club Press
an imprint of iUniverse.com, Inc.

For information address:
iUniverse.com, Inc.
620 North 48th Street, Suite 201
Lincoln, NE 68504-3467
www.iuniverse.com

ISBN: 0-595-12498-4

Printed in the United States of America

This book is the result of those who believed in me and those who doubted me. I thank you all.

1

A bright, happy sun glared down from its perch in the sky above, looking over a slow summer day. The glowing orb of gas peeked in and out of a series of wispy clouds. The clouds rode a strong breeze in a northeastern direction, gliding over fields of wheat and other grains. The quickly traveling cumulonimbus rose over a short hill, then spotted an oasis in the tan horizon. Speeding over first a cemetery, followed by a series of smaller houses, the clouds continued their unimpeded journey to the northeast. Below them, the monotony was broken by the occasional movement of sparse life, moving even slower than the day itself.

A small group of apartments accepted the shadows of the clouds as they passed over head. The clouds departed, allowing the sun to beat down on the tiny complex below. Despite the sun's warm rays, a crisp wind still gave the two-story buildings a cold shudder. The pale eggshell units were cut by the biting gale, their wooden decks beaten by the continuous pulsing, then ebbing, gusts. For early September, the climate of the sleepy town proved unseasonably cold.

Wooden steps creaked under the weight of two pairs of feet. The owner of the first set, a man in his mid-twenties, reached the top of the staircase. He turned to his companion, projecting his voice over the howling gust.

"Whoa! That breeze is gonna knock me over one a' these times!"

Barry Whipple stumbled with a cardboard box in both arms, struggling to position the weight of the box's contents as he fished for a ring of keys. He managed to slip two fingers of his left hand into the pocket of his gray Dockers and hooked the key ring, pulling it free. With his available fingers, Barry felt for the correct key on the ring. As he worked at his task, he tried to use his right toe to prop open the aluminum screen door that covered the prefabricated entrance. Still struggling with his task, Barry spotted a shadow on the ground as his companion reached the landing.

"Let me get that dear." Annie ducked her munchkinlike frame under Barry's raised arms. She opened the aluminum barricade, then twisted the door knob. The unlocked door resisted her hip check, but gave way under the duress. It yawned open to reveal the interior of the apartment.

Boxes upon coffins of cardboard littered the floor, stacked upon each other, waist high, throughout the living room of the apartment. A worn couch, decorated with a floral pattern, rested against the wall to the right. A hallway led to the left, guarded by boxes and an empty entertainment center. An oval table, covered in cardboard cubes, sat under a window in the farthest point from the front door. Its extra leaf was propped against the wall, beneath the legs of the table. Annie ventured into the clutter, following a path deliberately cleared during the transfer of boxes from truck to apartment. She cut to the left, moving down the short hallway.

Annie took four steps with her short legs, carrying a box marked "Kitchen" in her arms. She turned right at her first opportunity, then crossed over from brown carpet to bone-colored linoleum. Using whatever reserve strength she had, Annie lifted the hefty box with a forceful grunt and deposited it on the Formica counter. She wiped small drops of sweat from her forehead with purple sleeves. Returning to her task, she found a large kitchen knife and stabbed the packing tape holding shut the box. Successful in her attempt to puncture the tape, she tore the product from the lid, balled up the tape, and fired a turnaround jump shot into a waiting trash can.

Annie turned her attention back to the box, emptying Ziploc bags of silverware and plastic utensils from the cardboard sheath. Suddenly, she tensed and clutched at two hands that had interlocked around her slender waist. She felt a warm breath, then two moist lips pressed on her neck, just beneath her dishwater blonde hair, a short bob of a haircut. She tried to twist her neck to catch the sight of her attacker, but couldn't bend her head at the proper angle.

"What's that for?" she asked through a smile, struggling to regain the air that had been scared from her lungs.

"You looked beautiful standin' there, the sun glistening off your body," Barry replied, relinquishing his grip around her waist. Annie turned to face her husband.

"You know," Barry continued, "just cause we're back from Cancun doesn't mean the honeymoon has to end. I'd like to continue what we got started down there, if ya know what I mean."

"Yeah, I know what you mean," Annie responded, a sly, crooked smile crossing her lips. "Only one problem though."

"And what's that?" Barry removed his Ray-Bans. He grasped a loose tail of his red lumberjack shirt, carefully running the flannel material over the lenses to clean them.

"The bed's not here yet." Kate shrugged, the shadows around her making her look very disappointed.

Barry chuckled for a moment, his body pulsing with his laugh. He placed the black sunglasses on his face, adjusting them until they rested correctly across the bridge of his nose. "Tell you what. I'll go to Mom and Steve's and get another load while you start unpacking some a' our stuff here. When I get back, we'll…ah…crack the seal on this place."

"Okay. I guess," Annie replied, faking a yawn. She smiled again and ran her right hand across Barry's left temple and through his chocolate hair. She let the hand linger on his cheek, then whispered, in a breathless, sexy voice, "Hurry back." Barry backed into the hallway wall, quickly recovered, and worked his way through the menagerie of boxes to the front door. Annie listened to his fast steps as they echoed from the plywood stairs. Hearing the moving van roar to life in the parking lot, Annie pushed a now empty cardboard box to the floor. She kicked it powerfully, sending it bounding into the hallway to rest against the white wall. Turning her back to the scene, she returned to her task of sorting and storing the couple's kitchenware.

Annie moved around the kitchen at a breakneck pace, putting away items in various cupboards and drawers, both above her line of sight and below her waist. She unpacked a large stack of dish towels and laid them on the countertop. Scanning the kitchen briefly, Annie spotted one drawer she hadn't opened yet. Grabbing the golden plastic handle, Annie pulled forcefully toward herself. However, the drawer refused to budge. She shrugged her shoulders, followed by her wiping her fingertips on her denim jeans. She made a second attempt at the drawer, but found no success once more. Annie brushed goldenrod strands of hair from her eyes. A forced breath escaped her grinding teeth, followed closely by a light curse. She gathered herself, braced her right leg against a cabinet door, and, with a guttural groan, forced the drawer open.

Annie slipped the sleeves of her purple cotton sweatshirt above her elbows. Forcing another breath, she tucked off-color blonde locks behind her right ear. She looked into the now open prefabricated plywood drawer, finding the source of her difficulties.

"Hey, a notebook," she remarked to the quiet apartment. She lifted the bundle from its resting place. "It must've gotten caught in the top somehow. Whoever lived here before must've forgotten the thing."

Mrs. Whipple flipped the spiral notebook over in her hands until the beaten cover faced her. The cover, a heavy green sheet of paper, demonstrated considerable wear. A road map of wrinkles and tears crisscrossed the surface. A series of mostly incomplete doodles, in most cases partially finished faces, stared from the cover in an eternal gaze.

Through the damage, the words "My Journal" remained visible in black Magic Marker.

Annie shuffled to the nearby trash can. Holding the notebook over the waiting receptacle, she started to loosen her grip.

I wonder what this thing's about.

She reclaimed a solid grip on the journal, scooping it back into her steady grasp with an underhand motion. Notebook in hand, she exited the kitchen, turning left, toward the living room. She crossed the floor, then deposited her petite frame on the floral print couch.

Annie leafed open the notebook, immediately revealing a mahogany stain the approximate shape and size of a soda can. The first page, written in cursive handwriting, read, in its entirety:

The following is a journal meant to chronicle the most important periods in my life.

Annie furrowed her brow through clear bifocal lenses. She shrugged her shoulders and tucked a strand of dusty blonde hair behind her right ear. She crossed her right leg over her left and slid her hips forward. Reclining deeper into the cushions of the floral print couch, she carefully folded over the cryptic first page onto the wire spiral.

2

Sometimes in life an event, or series of events, happen and those who face them are never the same. I believe today, January 11, 1992, will prove to be one such event, a definition of life.

Ted sat alone in a small room, a tiny brick tomb inside a large brick tower. He leaned back in a tan recliner, sinking far deeper into the cushions than his six-foot-one, 150 pound frame should have. Through the flat, worn cushion, Ted could feel the hard surface of the floor, concrete beneath an ancient tawny carpet. His face wore a pained frown, and his hazel-blue eyes looked dark, distant, almost sunken in their sockets. He sighed deeply, but with a rush, making sure to keep the noise in check, to keep from drawing any unwanted attention.

Having just transferred to Eastern Washington University from community college, Ted had expected college life to be a little different. Instead of sitting in a bunker by himself on a Saturday night, Ted had imagined himself intoxicated at a party, be it at a house, a fraternity, or even an open field. He thought acceptance was automatic, that you received new friends along with your dormitory keys and financial aid check. He certainly hadn't envisioned the scene of him unpacking his belongings, then having his new roommate asking for the same boxes in order to pack up and leave. Some first week of college.

The picture on the television bounced and scrolled as a skit featuring the androgynous character Pat continued to play out to canned laughter from an unseen crowd. Usually "Saturday Night Live" helped Ted relax, but even his favorite television program did little to break him out of his funk. He stroked his chin, momentarily playing with the fuzzy, short whiskers he found. A quick glance at his watch led to a deep, open throated yawn. A commercial for a 900 party line flashed on the television screen as the picture began to bounce wildly. Static streamed through the screen, coinciding with a howling wind that could be heard crashing into the outside of the building.

I wish it would just snow already.

Ted wandered halfheartedly over to the 19-inch television console. He smacked the outer casing a few times with an open palm. Failing with this attempt, he opened a panel and fiddled with a series of knobs and buttons. At first the picture rolled, even more out of control than before, but it finally settled and held.

Ted returned to the brown chair, flopping carelessly into it. Immediately, a rush of pain invaded the back of his skull. Cursing through his lower lip, which he bit down on to suppress the pain, Ted spun to find the source of the attack, a chalk tray of a blackboard bolted to the wall behind him. Rubbing the wounded area, Ted returned to his intent stare toward the television.

Ted's icy stare pierced through the television into the wall itself. The only interruption in his focus was the occasional flicking of his tongue over his lips. He ignored the laughing voices on the program, preferring to count the number of bricks, from ceiling to floor, that made up the wall. He nearly finished counting when the heavy plywood door caved inward quickly. Ted snapped around, letting his right shoulder lead his neck, to see what caused the disturbance.

"Oh! Uh, I didn't expect anyone to be in here," remarked the first of a pair of girls. "You mind if we sit down?" she asked. Ted replied with a quick positive nod and a muttered "Go ahead" through tight lips, and the two girls entered, moving quickly left in front of Ted's seated position to a tattered couch in the corner.

The first girl tossed back her permed platinum blonde hair with her gloved hands. She dropped the ski gloves from her wrists, then slapped the surface of her lime green ski jacket with her naked palms and fingers. Water splashed off in tiny prismatic droplets, spraying lightly in all directions. Ted wiped clear the spray from both his face and pantleg, removing the moisture by running his hand over the armrest of the chair. The first girl unzipped her jacket, and asked, "Whatcha watchin'?" as she shook her shoulders free.

"'Saturday Night Live'," answered Ted. He cleared his throat and licked his lips.

"Has Pat been on yet?" The second girl spoke for the first time. She stood at least six inches shorter than her companion. They both weighed about the same; the first girl was waif thin, bordering on an anorexic condition. The second girl shook her fingers through her straight, shoulderlength hair, trying to shake dry her damp locks.

"Yeah. You just missed it." Ted's expression remained unchanged as he continued. "Is it snowing out?" His scowl momentarily disappeared, only to return in force as his voice trailed off.

"Snowing? No, we got into a snowball fight on our way home. It's too bad I missed Pat. She's my favorite." The second girl pulled her white windbreaker over her head. She shook her head, then ran her right hand through her curled bangs. The hand moved to the back of her head, checking to make sure an amber berette she found there still held her hair in check. Satisfied, she tossed her windbreaker on top of the first girl's ski jacket, using her left hand to guide the windbreaker to its resting place in the heap. Underneath the now removed windbreaker, the short girl wore a gray sweatshirt with "MHS Band" printed in green on the left breast.

Ted looked blankly at her for a moment, then turned his attention back to the television.

The two girls simultaneously sat on the couch. The couch, like the chair Ted occupied, gave way in the bottom more than it should have, and the girls slumped to the floor. They immediately lost themselves in a fit of giggles, rolling around the couch in a tangle of limbs until their faces flushed crimson. Ted smiled for a brief moment. He caught himself, fearing that someone might notice and think he actually found something enjoyable.

The girls regained their composure after a couple minutes. The shorter girl rested her arms on her thighs, smoothing out the wrinkles in her black slacks. She sat closest to Ted, whom she turned to and asked, "So…why weren't you at the dance?"

"I don't go to dances."

"Why not?" The girl leaned forward, and a scent that resembled fresh flowers filled Ted's nostrils.

"Look at me. Would you dance with me?"

"Point taken." Ted's eyes narrowed at the comment and a scowl that could break glass covered his face. It was met with a clever grin.

"Kidding! I'm kidding. Of course I would." Ted shifted in his chair as the girl continued. "Why would you say a thing like that?"

"Just experience I've had." Ted ran his right hand through his hair, pinkie finger following his part and thumb brushing past his ear. He then ran both hands through his week's growth of hair.

"Oh c'mon, it can't be *that* bad." The short girl paused for a moment, as if she expected to hear Ted's tale of woe. "Besides, now you've met me."

"True. I'm Ted."

"Hi Ted. I'm Kate…"

"And I'm Jenna," the first girl chimed in. She tossed back her scapula length hair. She leaned over and collected the respective coats. "Kate, it's gettin' kinda late and I need to work tomorrow. I'm goin' to bed." She handed Kate the balled-up windbreaker and pushed herself to her feet. Kate also rose from the seated position and headed for the door.

"Ted, I'll see you soon." Kate smiled at him and waved a timid hand from underneath her white wind jacket.

"Yeah, see ya later," Ted retorted, keeping his sarcasm as undetectable as possible. He shifted his hips, slumping still deeper into the dirty chair. The heavy door creaked shut, expelling a breath like a powerlifter does during a squat. The cold breath brushed Ted's neck, causing a light shudder.

About a half hour later, Ted prepared for bed. He grabbed his Reach toothbrush and wandered across the hallway from his dorm room. Entering the bathroom, he immediately heard a deep, nauseated cough followed by a splash, emanating from the far end of the restroom. Chuckling silently to himself, Ted stopped in front of the first sink. He pulled on the faucet, and lukewarm water poured from the spout. He squeezed Tartar Control Crest onto his brush, then pushed the instrument into his mouth. Ted quickly worked his way around his mouth, first over his upper molars and bicuspids, then the lower set of canines and incisors. Rinsing the toothbrush clean, Ted looked into the mirror. His eyes peered back at him, large and full of life. He blinked, then cupped his hands under the faucet, filling them with cool water. The water sloshed back and forth in Ted's mouth, then shot into the basin, propelled there by Ted's tongue.

Ted looked in the mirror again. As he stood there, a warm feeling began to push its way into his chest. His reflection lit up in the mirror and smiled. "Have a good evening!" Ted announced, greeted in response with a guttural heave. Ted spun on his heel, and, with toothbrush and Tartar Control Crest in hand, strutted out the door and across the hallway to his dormitory.

Before retiring for the evening, Ted fished through a drawer. He leafed past bank statements and fliers, Post-it notes and expired pizza coupons. At the bottom of the drawer, he found a clean, unused spiral notebook. He lifted it from the drawer and opened the green cover. Uncapping a Paper-Mate pen, Ted quickly scrawled down his thoughts about the events of the night, making sure to preserve every detail he could remember on the pages in sloppy cursive writing. Closing the cover, Ted sat in a dull, low light for a moment. He climbed to his feet, stepped to the vanity mirror, and removed his contact lenses. Placing them in their case, he looked briefly at his blurred image. A foggy grin, paled further by the dim lamp light, looked back at him.

Satisfied, he turned toward his bed, crawled under the sheets and blankets, and turned out the wall lamp.

3

February 4, 1992
I never really believed in God very much. He had never really done anything for me that proved he was trying to help me out. I think my thoughts on that subject are changing.

Ted wandered, sluggish, toward his mailbox. His mailbox was a small cube with a locking door on the front, one nondescript unit amongst the dozens that decorated the wall in the lobby that faced the elevators. Ted always enjoyed receiving a friendly letter or his weekly copy of *Sports Illustrated*, anything that could be a distraction from his mundane existence and prove to him that the outside world was thinking of him. He unlocked the door with his corresponding key. Reaching into Box 328, he found nothing. His perpetually tired look remained intact as he turned and dragged himself to the twin elevators. He pushed his hands into the front pockets of his jeans and rocked on his heels.

"Where's the damn elevator?" he muttered, barely audible over the hum of a nearby soda machine. He removed his hands from his pockets. Ted slid his sleeve above his elbow, uncovering his right wrist. Expecting to find his watch, Ted cursed silently when he found his arm bare. He flashed a quick glance at the sterile wall clock, then bore his glance into the elevator door in response to a grinding echo of a noise coming from the shaft. The cold gray steel parted, and a familiar face emerged and entered the lobby.

"Hey! Ted!" Kate enthusiastically announced, loud enough to turn heads. "Whatcha doin'?"

"Checkin' my mail," Ted replied. His low voice barely carried over the hum of the vending machine. "Where're you headed?"

"I was goin' to Tawanka for some deli."

"Have fun." Ted stepped toward the open elevator doors.

"Hey, come with me." Kate stopped his progress by clasping his left arm with her left hand. "You didn't eat already, didya?" She tightened her grip, squeezing his bicep lightly.

"No, I didn't eat yet," Ted lied, looking down at the skinny fingers wrapped around his underdeveloped musculature. Kate's grip subsided, and she released Ted's arm from her grasp. Ted studied her perfect fingernails, each covered in a clear polish and filed neatly. The hand worked its way past Kate's left ear, pushing a few strands of hair the color of wheat behind the lobe. Ted followed the path of Kate's hand, then focused on her eyes. Brilliant blue orbs looked back at him, blinking a couple times. Behind her, two heavy steel panels pressed together.

"Great. Let's go." Kate's lips moved with her words. Both lips were nicely proportionate; neither one dominated the other in the pair. Her upper teeth fit her mouth perfectly. Her lower teeth, while more crowded within their quarters than their upper counterparts, still looked very white and fresh.

Ted turned and walked with her, making sure his long gait compromised for her shorter choppy steps. They threw open the main doors, passed through a second, exterior set, and began walking down the hill toward the Eastern Washington University campus.

* * *

"A business major, huh? So you've already decided?" Kate carried the majority of the conversation. Ted preferred to listen to her sweet, soft voice, to watch her facial expressions change.

"Yeah. I mean…I…think that's what I want to do." Ted scratched his scalp, then shifted his attention to his left wrist. "What about you?"

"I'm not too sure. I haven't decided yet. I need to pretty soon though."

"How come?"

"My parents. They want me to figure it out. That's kinda why I'm here."

The two of them stopped at a four way intersection. They waited on the curb for an accordion bus to rumble by, then they scrambled across the intersection diagonally with a half trot, half sprint. They hopped the curb, and they once more slowed to a deliberate pace.

Kate continued her explanation. "I'm from Spokane. I live in the dorms only 'cause I wanted out of my parents' house."

"Me too. I came here from Olympia because I wanted to get away from everyone. I couldn't stand being stuck in the same rut my high school friends were in. I wasn't gonna be stuck stocking diapers at Target, livin' with my parents, hanging out downtown Friday night. I want more than that."

"I know. One quarter at community college was all I could take. I had to be here." The two of them stopped at another curb, met by a two-lane road. They checked both ways, crossed the street, and wound slightly left, toward the campus.

Nearly every building surrounding the main courtyard on Eastern's campus was erected with brick. To break the rusty bleakness, whoever designed the campus tried to retain as many trees as possible. Bare branches reached for sunlight; piles of leaves littered the road map of sidewalks that passed beneath them. Rapidly evaporating puddles provided the only remnants of the winter's snowfall. A few brave students wore shorts, others no jackets, definitely a rarity for early February in eastern Washington. A light breeze tickled the backs of Ted and Kate's necks as they walked across the courtyard, in front of Patterson Hall, to the Tawanka Commons.

Tawanka Commons stood out among its brick brethren. The exterior of the building was a pale eggshell color, covered in a gravelly stucco material. Most of the other buildings were three to four stories high, while Tawanka checked in at barely two. Finally, panes of glass allowed natural light into the building, whereas the other structures were decorated, for the most part, with sparse, small windows. Ted pushed open the first of two sets of doors. Kate followed closely behind, and the two acquaintances passed into a foyer.

They encountered a short hallway, then a wall decorated with a glass display case. The hall split in two directions, left and right. Ted and Kate stepped into the intersection and studied signs that hung from the ceiling and were illuminated in red. Kate pointed to the sign in the hallway to the left, which indicated that the deli line was open. Kate led the way down the short corridor, around a corner right, and through a longer hallway to a flight of stairs at the back of the building. They climbed two sets of stairs, then entered a small room occupied by a single woman seated behind a cash register. Kate passed her student identification to the lady while Ted fumbled his from his wallet. After they were both docked points from their meal plans with a quick swipe of a wand over a bar code, the two new friends entered the vacant deli line, Ted in the lead, Kate close behind.

"So what do you want?" The deli worker, a short man with dark hair, stared blankly at Ted.

"Hell, I don't know what you have," grumbled Ted. "I've never been here before."

"We have deli stuff," calmly responded Deli Boy.

"And what the hell is that?" Ted barked. The lady from behind the cash register craned her head around the corner, peeking from behind Kate's shoulder.

"You know, meat an' stuff." Deli Boy's fingers wiggled inside clear plastic gloves.

"Oh. Very clear of you." Ted's lips curled into a scowl.

"Ted, get chicken or turkey. It's the best thing they have here." Kate quietly inched forward, making the impression to the small crowd behind them that the line was, in fact, moving.

"Oh. Okay, um…I'll have…a…turkey sandwich." Ted struggled to choke out the words. He cast his eyes toward the linoleum tile and his black Adidas shelltoes.

"Whatta you want on it?" Deli Boy asked in a confident voice.

"No mayonnaise," Ted answered softly, wiping light beads of sweat from his brow. Deli Boy piled on lettuce, tomatoes, sprouts, and onions, slapped mustard on the white bread, and hastily sliced the sandwich in half diagonally. He slid the plate to Ted and went to work on Kate's turkey on white, nodding without looking up when Ted thanked him.

Ted and Kate each placed their sandwiches on trays and passed into the dining hall. They immediately moved left to a bank of soda machines. Ted filled a glass with Coca-Cola, Kate with Sprite. They stopped, looked over the cafeteria, and walked slowly to the center of the structure.

The cafeteria spread out in front of them in a series of vertical rows. Each row was created by two long tables pushed together. Each table featured a bench bolted to each side. Four people could comfortably occupy each bench, so it was possible for as many as 16 people to sit at each vertical column. Most of the tables were filled, all of them with strange people with unfamiliar faces. Kate extended a pinkie from the bottom of her tray, muttered "Over there", and began to wander toward the booths.

The booths set up beyond the long rectangular tables. Beyond the booths, barely visible from the position Kate and Ted maintained, sat a series of round tables. Kate's movement indicated she planned to find an open booth, and she soon found one to her liking. She squeezed into the seat, sliding across red vinyl until she reached a comfortable spot. Letting her posture relax slightly by pressing her shoulders lightly on skinny wooden slats, she exhaled and picked up a half of her turkey sandwich.

Ted squirmed awkwardly into the booth from the other side. Kate bit into her sandwich, then put the meal on her tray. She swallowed the piece of flesh in her mouth, looked at Ted for a second, and began to giggle with a snort of air through her nose.

Ted stared coldly through her. "What's so funny?" he asked, picking lettuce and sprouts from his turkey on white and depositing them in a neat pile on the tray.

"I'm sorry," Kate laughed. "I mean, c'mon, that was pretty funny back there."

"Huh," Ted grunted, biting into his sandwich.

"You don't think so?" Kate looked up from her meal, waiting for a response. "I mean, think about it. It was pretty funny."

"Uh…yeah, I guess," Ted replied, then thought for a moment. He put down his sandwich half, looking at Kate. They made eye contact, saying nothing. After a shared breath, they both snorted into a long belly laugh. Ted tried to hide his face from the prying eyes of those around the duo. The two new friends both covered their mouths with their hands, but it didn't muffle the noise.

*   *   *

"So, what's your family like?" Kate and Ted hopped down the second flight of stairs, but the question stopped Ted on the middle landing.

"You really want to know?"

"Yeah, of course. I wouldn't ask if I didn't. What're they like?"

Ted bounded to the floor and rejoined the simple pace the two of them shared. "Well…my dad's a doctor. He works in the emergency room, basically twelve hours every day. He done a lot more than that though. He served two tours of duty in Vietnam in the late 60's. He ran marathons for awhile, even the Boston Marathon in '78 or '79, I can't remember which. My dad's really a great guy."

"Interesting. So...I guess your parents are divorced."

Ted backed into the outer door, pushing it open and using his weight to hold it for Kate. "What? Oh, no! They're happily married. Why'd you think that?"

"Well, I asked about your family, but you only talked about your dad." Kate pushed stray strands of hair behind her ear, fighting a gentle breeze with her effort.

"My fault. I'm just closer to my dad. I think it's 'cause I got the name he wanted."

"Do what?" Kate stopped for a second, the confusion on her face amplified by her squinting in the glare of the sunlight beating off the pavement.

"Well, Dad got to choose my name, so I'm Theodore Roosevelt after his favorite president. My mom got to name my brother, so he's John Kennedy."

Satisfied with the explanation, Kate regained her stride. The two friends worked their way through the growing sea of students and up the steady incline toward Morrison Hall. The wall of coeds slowly decreased as they approached the dormitory. As they reached the entrance, a skinny arm reached into the sky and a taller girl approached from the right.

"Kate! Kate!" It was Jenna. "Kate! Hold up!"

"Wassup girl?" Kate replied.

"Nothin'. I, uh, saw Bart a bit ago."

"Hm. How lucky for you." She flashed a glance in Ted's direction. "You remember Ted, right?"

"Oh yeah, of course. How ya doin' Ted?" Jenna twirled a necklace with her right index finger. She rubbed the charm with her finger and thumb. Ted blinked as the sun gleamed off the charm, a half-circle with a jagged right side. The name Bart still echoed in his ears.

"Me? I'm pretty good," Ted replied, his voice trailing off.

"Don't you hafta work today Jenna?" Kate asked.

"Yep. That's where I was headed." Jenna took a step backward. "You gonna be around tonight?"

"Yeah, I'll be here," Kate replied.

"I'll come by later. Ted, good seein' you again." Jenna started to climb a nearby hill toward the parking lot.

"See ya." Ted waved his hand, then let it drop by his side.

The two friends entered the building together and moved toward the elevators in the lobby. Most of the crowd had dissipated, so getting on the elevator took little effort. The doors shut and they began to rise toward their respective floors.

"Could you push three?" they asked an Asian girl, in unison. Ted's mouth momentarily hung open.

My God! She lives on my floor!

The elevator gasped open, revealing the lobby of the third floor. Tawny carpet extended across the floor, covering every square millimeter in a putrid orange-brown material. Couches made of a weak wood fiber, not much above balsa on the evolutionary chain, formed a square around a low table. Ted and Kate passed the couches and exited into the north side of the third floor.

Two hallways created a fork at the entrance. One hallway led left at a precise 90 degree angle; the other corridor snaked right about five feet, then pushed straight ahead. Ted moved left, Kate right. Ted stopped at the last door on the left in his short hallway.

The key slid into the door, and with a simple twist of the knob the door creaked ajar. Ted dropped his ring of keys on the dresser and scooped up a stack of newspapers that had collected on the second mattress. Unlike most people in the dorms who enjoy the luxury of no roommate, Ted opted not to stack both mattresses together, choosing instead to use the second bed like a love seat. He looked into the vanity mirror mounted over the dresser. "My hair sure sucks," he mumbled to a poster of Frank Thomas, keeping a sharp eye on his reflection.

Dropping the newspapers back onto the bed, Ted licked his fingers and worked his hands through his hair.

After admiring his self improvement, Ted lifted his keys from their resting place on the dresser top. He forced the ring into his pocket, turned on his left toe, and stopped.

Kate stood in his archway, her weight shifted subtly on her right leg. Sunlight playfully glistened in her hair, creating an angelic corona of light around her head. Her stance was almost seductive, but still innocent.

"You play tennis?" she asked matter-of-factly, as if the question at hand was the logical next step in their conversation. She pulled up her sleeves with her dainty fists.

"Sure, I can play," Ted replied. "Or, at least I can fake like I can."

"Good," she laughed. "So, you wanna play with me?"

You don't know how bad.

"Yeah! That sounds cool."

"Great. Let's go." Kate started to turn to leave.

"Um, maybe we should call ahead. I don't know if we need to reserve a court or not." Ted grabbed a phone directory for the campus and surrounding town, picking it up from the spare bed.

"Good idea."

Ted called the athletic facility and learned that none of the courts were available. He suggested continuing their earlier conversation in the lobby. He followed Kate down the hall and to the square of couches in the elevator lobby. Kate eased onto one cushion, carefully positioning her weight evenly before sitting. Ted flopped sloppily into a slouched position, then pushed himself up by planting his soles firmly on the carpet and extending his legs. They continued talking, eventually exhausting the daylight.

4

February 29, 1992
Good thing there was a leap year this year. It gave me an extra day to be around Kate.

Twin elevator doors yawned open, releasing a scurry of shuffling feet. A half dozen coeds dispersed, some toward the front exit of the building, others toward the wall of mailboxes. One soul stepped quickly to the left, stopping in front of a vending machine.

Ted scratched his chin as he perused the selection of candy confections contained in the vending machine. Bright colored wrappers full of sugary taste faced him, just out of reach behind a thick pane of glass. Ted read the various prices while flipping unseen money inside the pocket of his jeans. He spotted the item he craved, a Peanut Butter Twix. Producing a folded dollar bill from his pocket, Ted flattened the bill and loaded it into the machine.

Contrary to every other first attempt with the vending machine, the bill slid into the slot and loaded on the first try.

Ted repeated the letter and number combination in his mind as he punched the letter B and the number six into the keypad. *My favorite vitamin* he thought as he entered the combination. A whirring of gears, and the candy bar with the crispy cookie center dropped into a collection tray at the bottom of the machine with a hollow thump. Ted bent over at the waist and extended his left hand into the bin.

A second, similar noise to the hollow thump echoed inside the bin.

Ted fished around the bin with his left palm, coming across the source of the noise. Pulling his hand free, he looked with amazement at the treasure that had been produced. Instead of one Peanut Butter Twix, Ted had cheated the system and found himself clutching two candy bars. "Sweet!" he commented to the vending machine. Ted turned to leave.

"Excuse me," a strange voice called from an unseen vantage point to Ted's right. Ted twisted on his right heel, turning to face the deep voice.

"How you doin'?" a blonde man with a goatee asked, standing with his right foot on flat carpeting and his left foot on the tile floor. The figure standing before Ted reminded him of the Nazi ideal: blonde thatch of hair, blue eyes, and muscular build. The man was a chiseled specimen, confident enough in his body to wear a white tank top. The tank top covered a thick chest and a tight set of abdominals which rippled through the fabric. His striated shoulders spilled forth from the garment. Large biceps and triceps led to a pair of thick forearms. His forearms flexed as he gripped a pool cue with both hands.

"Fine," Ted replied, pulling the sleeves of his sweatshirt over his featureless forearms.

"Hey, do you know how to play pool? I'll play you if you're interested."

"I haven't really played very much, but okay."

"Great." The physical wonder strode to a table around the corner from the vending machine, carried by legs that bulged beneath blue jeans. He bent at the waist, picking up a triangle of plastic from the floor. Ted followed him to the table, propelled by his stick figure legs.

Ted pushed all 15 balls into the rack, making sure a colored ball was in every corner, the one ball in front. He shifted balls around, making sure that the eight ball found its way to the center and a solid, stripe, solid, stripe, solid pattern made up the perimeter of the rack. Sliding the rack forward to a circular mark on the table, he tightened the rack with his fingers and lifted the triangle away. Looking up, Ted said, "Hey. My name's Ted."

"Pleased to meet you Ted. I'm Bart."

Ted studied his new acquaintance for a moment, then dropped the triangle to the carpet. He grabbed a second pool cue and ground blue chalk onto the tip as Bart started the game. A ferocious collision of pool cue against cue ball sent the white sphere crashing into the rack. Balls, both striped and solid, careened from the tight rack, heading on 16 separate journeys around the table. The four dropped into the far left corner pocket, while the cue spun off the nine and toward the left rail. It rested a few inches from the rail, far enough to get a clear shot at the two.

Bart slithered to the far side of the table, sizing up his shot at the two ball. Brimming with confidence at the sight of the straight shot, he slipped the pool cue between his left index and middle fingers. The cue ball glided across green felt, kissing the two ball before bouncing off the short rail and back toward the center of the table. The two disappeared into darkness.

Ted stepped toward the other end of the table as Bart looked over his next shot from the short end of the playing surface. Bart saw two options: the one ball, within a reasonable distance from the center right pocket; and the seven, also near the center of the table but only able to fall if it reached the right corner pocket. Bart silently calculated the angle to cut the one ball, and, with a flick of his thick right wrist, sent the cue ball colliding with it. The one ball immediately dropped, but the cue ball rolled unimpeded toward the left corner pocket. It brushed the inside right of the pocket and slipped down the hole. "Damn. Scratched," Bart grumbled as Ted waited for the cue ball to roll into a slot built into the base of the pool table.

Ted surveyed his seven striped balls as he searched for a spot to place the cue ball. Choosing to go after the 13, which waited near the right corner pocket, Ted lined up the two balls and stabbed at the cue ball. It hit the 13 squarely, knocking it from the field of play as it ducked down the pocket. "Nice shot," Bart deadpanned as Ted eyed the 15 ball. He stroked the cue, but his shot encountered the six on its way and fell off line. "Your shot," Ted countered, and Bart studied the situation briefly before smoking the six into the near right corner.

* * *

"So Ted, what floor do you live on?" Bart asked, chalking up his stick. He looked at a table littered with striped balls and sparsely populated with solid colored spheres.

"I live up on the third floor. How 'bout you?"

"Me? Oh, I live on five." Bart lined up his shot, the three in the right corner. He smoothly pushed the pool cue against the cue ball, sending it into his intended target. The three approached the pocket, rattled around the padded brim, and popped back out. "Damn," Bart growled, stepping back from the table as Ted peered over the five balls he had remaining.

"So, you live on the third floor huh? I have a girlfriend who lives up there." Bart leaned against the brick wall, watching Ted size up a shot at the 14 ball.

"Huh. Amazing what a small world we live in." Ted calmly knocked the 14 into the far left corner pocket. The cue ball drifted back to the center of the table.

"Yeah, she's great. She's the perfect girl for me. She pretty much lets me do whatever I want."

Ted deposited the 12 in the far side pocket. The cue stopped in perfect position to remove the 15 from the field of play.

"I mean," Bart continued, "she doesn't even know about the other girl I'm dating right now. In fact, I saw both of them yesterday without either one knowing."

"You should watch yourself my friend. She's probably smarter than you give her credit for." Ted smashed the 15 into the pocket closest to his left. The cue ball rebounded from the rail, traveling into the far rail and back toward the pocket to Ted's right. The ten waited in the far right corner.

"Nah. I've been dating women behind her back for a few months now. She hasn't caught on yet. Why would she now?"

Ted lined up the ten in the right corner. Stroking the cue smoothly, he followed through with a touch of finesse. The cue ball clattered off the ten, which immediately dropped. The cue bounced off the rail, crossing green felt until it slowly rolled to a halt near the center of the table. Only three balls remained: the three, resting on the short rail to Ted's left; the 11, about three inches outside the center pocket on the far side of the table from Ted; and the eight, directly in the path between the cue ball and the 11.

Ted leaned over the table for a closer look. Lifting his eyes to make contact with Bart's cocky gaze, Ted asked, "Don't you think that maybe she might get tired of you and leave you for someone else? You know, some guy could just sweep her right out from under your nose."

"Nope. Won't happen. I'm always the one who does the breaking up. Besides, she'd be nowhere without me."

"Okay." Ted looked over the table a second longer. "Oh, what's the rule about the eight ball? Can I hit it into the 11?"

"No. You can't hit the eight ball first."

"Fair enough. I'm gonna come off this rail over here then." Ted took a skip step, then hopped around to the other side of the table. From his position, his only shot at the 11 was to knock the cue ball off the rail and push the 11 into the side pocket directly in front of him. He leaned over to inspect the shot.

Ted calmly slid the pool stick between his fingers twice. A smile crossed his lips as he struck the cue ball. The white sphere collided with the far rail and bounced off toward the near side pocket. It cracked the

11 and instantly stopped. Ted lifted his left leg from the carpet, coaxing the 11 to the pocket. The 11 was running out of steam rapidly, but the ball was on line to fall in the near side pocket.

As it reached the pocket, it slowed to the point where it clung to the edge of the pocket, needing a half a rotation more to drop.

The 11 moved one more rotation. Ted shuffled on his toes like a prizefighter, pinwheeling the pool cue in his hands as he skipped to the short side of the table.

Bart looked toward a stairwell behind Ted, responding to a shuffle of feet on the tiled steps. "Hey Ted, there's my girlfriend I was telling you about," he nodded, directing Ted's attention to the approaching figure. Ted turned to his right, immediately casting his gaze on Kate as she reached the top of the stairs.

Kate struggled with a backpack as she walked at a brisk pace past the pool table and toward the lobby. When she reached the two men, she was greeted by a harmonious chorus of "Hey Kate." She slowed her steps, shifting her glare from the floor to her right and focusing on her two greeters.

She flashed a separate quick glance at each man and responded.

"Hey Ted."

Bart took a step toward her, pool cue in hand, but Kate resumed her fast pace and disappeared beyond the vending machine. Ted called out "Eight ball, corner pocket!" and pounded the cue ball into the eight, sending it on a direct path to the far left corner pocket. The black ball slipped from view as Ted tossed the stick onto the felt-covered table. "Thanks for playing me, Bart."

"What? You beat me?" Bart stood with pool cue in beefy hand, his mouth hanging half open. He looked like he was trying to divide 286 by 13.

"Looks like it. I'm gonna go catch up with my friend Kate. I'll see you around." Ted jogged in the direction of the elevators.

Bart remained astounded by the turn of events. "Yeah. I'll...I'll see ya around. Thanks for playing." He bent at the knees, peering into the shadowy slot to retrieve the 14 balls not already on the table.

Ted chose the stairs instead of the elevator. He ran through Second North, reaching the stairwell at the back of the building. He sprinted up two flights of stairs until he reached the third floor, which he exited onto. Slowing to a walk, he stopped in the corridor when Kate stepped into the hallway.

"Hey Kate," he said in an exuberant voice.

"Hey Ted," she returned, in a barely audible, low voice. Her voice, contrary to Ted's brisk, upbeat tone, sounded tired and ragged. She turned left into an adjoining hallway. Ted followed her to her dormitory room.

Ted stood with his left shoulder against the doorjamb as Kate sat on her bed. "Can I talk to you a minute?" he asked, rubbing his chin with his left hand.

"Sure. What about?"

"I just thought you should know about what Bart is doing behind your back."

"Oh. Don't worry, I know. I mean, a trained chimp would know he's cheating on me."

"Then why do you still date him? I mean, why did you see him yesterday, for example?"

Kate's mouth turned down in an ugly frown. "Did he tell you that?"

"Yeah. It didn't happen?"

"I guess if he considers saying hello to me in the lobby seeing me, then yes."

Ted slipped both hands into the front pockets of his blue jeans. "So...why do you let him treat you like that?"

"I don't any more. You know, I liked him at first, until he got here last fall and started having less time for me. It didn't take much for me to figure out what he's been up to here. I've been distancing myself from him for months. He's just too dumb to get the clue."

Ted smiled at Kate's comment. "What, him dumb? No, I don't see that."

Kate laughed at the sarcasm in Ted's voice. "You know, even though he's a bastard, I still liked being with him more than being alone."

"Kate, I don't think you should worry about that. You'll find a better guy, and I bet it's sooner than later."

"Thanks Ted."

"You're welcome." Ted shifted his weight from his left leg, propped against the doorjamb, to an even position. "I'm gonna go now. I just wanted to say 'hi' to you." He turned and began to head down the hallway, to the right. A wrapper crinkled between his fingers as he tore open a Peanut Butter Twix.

"Ted?" Kate called, which served to stop Ted before he got started.

"Yes Kate?"

"Did you beat him?"

"I sure did. And I'm not sure what was best about it, the way I beat him or the fact he's downstairs right now trying to figure out how I did it."

"Glad to hear it. Maybe that'll slow him down. Thanks."

Ted reached out and grasped the door knob of Kate's room, pulling the door silently shut behind him as he turned and wandered toward his own dorm room. He bit into the Peanut Butter Twix, letting his taste buds play with the combination of chocolate, peanut butter, and cookie before swallowing.

Kate kicked her penny loafers from her feet and rolled to her stomach, to lie down for a nap. She caught herself with her palms before her face impacted her pillow.

Waiting on her down pillow, like a mint on a hotel comforter, was an unopened package, wrapped in foil. Kate picked up the package, tore open the foil, and snacked on the Peanut Butter Twix contained inside the wrapper.

5

April 11, 1992
She must be someone important in my life. Geoff doesn't like her in the least.

Ted stood in front of the vanity mirror, then slid open one half to expose a medicine cabinet. He pawed around inside, didn't find what he wanted, and closed the left side. Opening the right, he instantly spotted a small bottle of ointment. He grasped the canister and slid the mirrored partition back into place. The overhead lamp crackled and buzzed to life, the result of a round button being pressed in.

Ted could hardly recognize himself through the mess his face had become. A brown, dry scab extended across his visage, from one cheek across the bridge of his nose and to the other cheekbone. The entire monstrosity stretched about an inch tall on average, growing thicker on the cheeks and thinner across the bridge. In a way, the scab resembled the logo of Batman.

Ted squinted at his reflection, hoping to crack the misshapen skin; he achieved his goal, producing tiny fissures and fault lines. Carefully scratching at a few areas, Ted was able to peel small flakes of browned skin away. He finished his careful task and twisted off the ointment's lid. He squeezed a few dabs of the creamy substance from the tube and applied the medicine to his injuries. Ted covered the affected area, then screwed the lid back on the tube. The tube of cream ended up on the dresser's flat surface, tossed nonchalantly on top of a thin phone directory. With a final, quick inspection, Ted turned and dropped onto the wrinkled sheets of his unmade bed. He slid himself up to two flattened pillows, pushed himself onto his side, and closed his eyes.

Thoughts and questions of all types flooded his head, but gradually they all left his consciousness except for the thoughts of Tucson, Arizona. Ted had decided to venture to that oasis to attend Spring Training. His planning began in early February, and in late March, during Spring Break, he made the journey. He had two motives when he arrived in Tucson: one, to watch some baseball games; two, to catch up with Shawna.

Ted spent his senior year in high school tiptoeing around the raven-haired beauty in blue jeans. He did gain enough courage during that year to ask her to the Senior Prom, which she happily agreed to attend. The image of crimson material against her alabaster skin still gave Ted a thrill whenever he thought of it. As the isolation of living in Cheney grew more unbearable with each passing day, Ted decided to stem the tide by connecting with Shawna once again.

The first two days in Tucson went according to Ted's preconceived plans. Ted spent the bulk of the daylight at Hi Corbett Field watching the Cleveland Indians prepare for the upcoming season. He took time out of each day to eat at the local mall's food court, then he shut himself in his hotel room at night. Being too young to rent a car, Ted relied on his feet for transportation. Being too young to think clearly all the time, Ted neglected to prepare for the desert sun. Both indiscretions became painfully obvious on the third day.

Ted carried high hopes with him as he left the Aztec Inn that day. His plan was to leave the game that afternoon and walk to the University of Arizona, visit Shawna, and return to his hotel later, on foot. A good plan, but Ted fell victim to cruel circumstances along the way.

Even before he left Hi Corbett Field, the trouble commenced. Ted held a continuous squint under the bright Sonorrhan sunlight throughout the early afternoon. No matter what he tried, he found no relief for the great warmth he felt on his face. A splash of water. A couple of ice cubes. Nothing helped.

Ted wandered out of the stadium and began his trek. He figured, judging by a map in the phone book he studied briefly a few short hours before, that the walk would take about fifteen minutes before he reached his destination. Slowly, then wearily, Ted stumbled on through the unrelenting sun, finding nothing but tan and tawny dirt and sizzling blacktop. Every block felt like three, every three blocks like descending into another level of Dante's version of Hell. What few buildings Ted found through his swollen eyes seemed to mock him, giving him hope while playing their cruel joke. Finally, mercifully and after an hour of walking, Ted spotted an immense structure on the right. Other buildings loomed around Arizona Stadium, but the stadium was the oasis of hope on the otherwise barren landscape.

Ted was waved across a side street by a girl with a pretty smile. She brushed her fair skinned fingers through her midnight black hair, then sped away in her green Chevy Celebrity. Ted trotted to the other curb, running with high knees and a straight back. He skipped once as he reached the grass. He wandered onto the campus, and, without much trouble, located the twin dormitories, Apache and Santa Cruz.

Security measures on the Arizona campus were much tighter than at Eastern. Ted waited patiently under the shadow cast by the building until three girls opened the locked doors. He flashed a quick smile, then winced, as he held open the heavy door for the ladies. They thanked him as they stepped out. Ted nodded a "No problem" to them and scurried into the building.

He scrambled up a series of stairs to the third floor. Even in the low light, Ted still squinted, but he seemed to know where to go. On a hunch, he turned right and walked slowly, confidently, down the hallway.

Arriving at room 319, Ted took a series of deep breaths, then knocked forcefully on the hard door.

No answer.

Ted knocked again, more meekly, and waited. He licked his fingertips and combed them through his hair. Fishing in his pockets, he produced a scrap of paper and a pen. He began to scribble a note when he heard giggling coming from the direction of the stairwell.

Ted turned to face the laughter, puffing his chest, straining to make his eyes as wide as possible. Three girls emerged from the stairwell, each one brilliantly blonde. Ted returned to his note, stopping to give the girls a "Hey" as they passed him in the hallway. They returned a cordial greeting, then disappeared around a bend in the hallway to Ted's left.

Looking at the door in front of him, Ted stopped his chicken scratches and allowed his eyes to relax. He thought about how far he had come in the past six months. As he closed his aching eyelids, a figure of his future appeared in his mind. There, in his thoughts, he caught a vision of a girl, a short girl, a blonde with an incredible grin and a strong energy. Opening his eyes, Ted from Olympia looked down at his hastily thrown together notes and watched as Ted from Cheney crumbled that scrap of paper in his fist and pushed it into the hip pocket of his khaki shorts. Ted turned his back to the door and retraced his steps to the stairwell. Within a couple minutes, he reemerged from Santa Cruz Hall, once again immersed in the intense sunlight.

"Why didn't I leave that note?" Ted mumbled to no one. Ted stood behind a desk chair. In his hands he held a photo album. He briefly leafed through the cardboard pages, stopping at random photographs of baseball players, sometimes touching the clear plastic that protected the images. Closing the burgundy cover, he dropped the album gingerly onto the countertop. Ted ran his fingers through his hair, then brushed his right hand over his injured nose. He glanced to his left, catching another glimpse of his reflection. Resisting the urge to scratch at his disfigurement, Ted returned to his photo album, lifting open the burgundy cover.

A knock at the door broke his concentration. Ted closed the photo album and tossed it on an upper shelf while turning toward the door. He took a step forward, then stopped as the door yawned open.

"Geoff," Ted said. He felt a cold spot of goo on his left cheek and rubbed the ointment into his skin.

"Ted. Always a pleasure." Geoff's narrow eyes peered from underneath the bill of a red baseball cap, pulled low over his scalp. "What's up cuz?" he continued, tossing a black duffel bag onto the extra mattress.

"I was waiting for you, you goof. It's about time you got here."

"Yeah, I see you cleaned up for me," replied Geoff, shoving aside newspapers as he sat on the spare mattress.

"Nice." Ted scooped up the newspapers, then deposited the stack on his bed, resting them on unmade sheets and a damp white towel. "How was your flight?"

"Thank *God* it's over! I thought we were gonna crash the whole time." Geoff shrugged his St. Louis Cardinals jacket from his shoulders. He followed by removing his red cap, exposing a cinnamon skullcap of growth.

"What, you didn't like Empire?" Ted chuckled as he spoke.

"You mean Empire. Empire! EMPIRE!" Geoff replied, each repetition of the word made deeper and bolder by his husky voice.

"You saw the barfbags too?"

"Saw them? I thought I'd probably need to use about three of them." Geoff giggled, producing one from his coat pocket. "I may still need one after lookin' at this place."

"Ah, c'mon now. It's not that bad."

"Well, it's not your bedroom back home."

"Nice." Ted grabbed a black hooded sweatshirt from the closet. "You hungry?"

"Always." Geoff patted his stomach as proof.

"Well, you're in for a treat." Ted pulled the sweatshirt over his head. "We're goin' for Squirtburgers!"

"For what?" Geoff slung his jacket around his back, pushing first his left arm and then his right into the sleeves.

"Squirtburgers. They're like regular hamburgers, only with…I don't know…special…squirty…ness." Ted slid his arms in the sleeves of his sweatshirt.

"You make it sound so good."

"Hey, have I ever let you down?"

"No .. oh, wait. There was that one time." Geoff slapped his hat back on his head, using both hands to get the curvature of the brim at an acceptable angle.

"Would you just come on already?" Ted grabbed his key ring from atop the dresser, then ushered Geoff into the hallway.

"Oh, hey. You remember that girl Kate I told you about?"

"You mean the short blonde?"

"Yeah. Her. Well, she's in two of my classes this quarter!" Ted's chest expanded, his voice reflecting total confidence.

"Well good, Maybe you'll get with 'er now."

Yeah maybe. With any luck.

* * *

Ted spent much of the next three days serving as Geoff's personal tour guide, showing him around both Cheney and Spokane. Ted made sure to attend his classes, but he let school slip into a secondary role beyond that. On Wednesday afternoon, a hollow knock came on his door. The door opened, and Kate appeared in the open space.

"Hey! What's up Kate?" Ted pronounced happily, gulping down a sip of soda as he did.

"Have you worked on the astronomy assignment yet?" Kate asked, sliding her left hand up her leg.

"Haven't even started yet," Ted replied matter-of-factly. "Gonna finish it tonight though."

"Great." Kate shifted her weight to her right leg. "Think we could work on it together?" She nibbled softly on her left index finger for a moment.

"That would be great," Ted replied. He heard a long, deliberate sigh, then quickly recovered. "Oh, Kate? This is my cousin Geoff."

"Hey Geoff."

"Hi." Geoff waved his right hand halfheartedly from his spot on the extra bed. Kate couldn't see his face, which was concealed behind the dresser.

"Okay. See you about seven o'clock tonight then." Kate turned and started to pull the door closed, then released the knob. Another arm, this one thicker and butterscotch in color, pushed the door open.

"Ted, wassup?" Maceo entered the room. Maceo wore his sweatpants low, beneath his thick belly. His hands were buried inside the waist band, doing things only Maceo knew for sure. His fireplug chest expanded with his next breath. "Can I borrow your TLC?"

"Up there," Ted replied, waving a finger toward his compact disc collection on a distant high shelf. "Hey, when'm I gettin' my Mary J. Blige back?"

"Marcie's got it. Ask her." Maceo picked up the jewel case and examined the interior. Satisfied that the correct disc was in there, he closed the case. "Oh, Bobby Brown too?"

"In the player." Ted rolled over to face Maceo.

Maceo began to leave, but he stopped at the door. "So...I saw your little friend leaving here. When are you gonna get with that?"

"It ain't like that."

"Maybe not...but it could be. You got that wide open."

"Don't play me," Ted replied, sitting up on the bed.

"Alright. But if I was you, I'd hit it and quit it." Maceo disappeared down the hallway, compact discs in his meaty hands.

"That was Maceo," Ted explained to Geoff. "I told you a little about him before."

"Uh huh. I met him yesterday. He asked for your paper."

"Yeah. He's my Negro Amigo." They both laughed, then continued eating and talking.

* * *

"Okay, listen to this." Ted licked his lips briefly, then continued. "According to the book, luminosity is the real or absolute brightness of a star, the total rate at which it radiates energy. Luminosity is directly related to temperature, the hotter the brighter. That answers question four."

"Hey, good. Now…could you repeat that again, only slow enough for us normal people to understand?" Kate uncapped her pen, pulling off the cap with her teeth.

"Yeah Ted. You're a son of a bitch." Geoff spoke in a throaty, scratchy voice, like an elderly gentleman.

"No. You're a son of a bitch."

"You're a bully." Geoff continued his grampa voice.

"No, you're a bully." The two cousins shared a laugh, Geoff leaning back in the desk chair until he lost his balance. He regained composure just before pitching over to the floor, catching himself by propping his back against the brick wall that created the closet.

"Do what?" Kate asked, on the outside looking at an inside joke.

"I think I'm gonna wet my pants," Geoff snorted, his voice about one octave higher than usual.

"We saw two old guys on the bus arguing yesterday," Ted explained through a giggle. "Funnier than a good kick in the pants."

"I…see…I think."

"Don't worry about it," Geoff answered. "After all, we're just a couple of dorks."

"You've got that half right." Kate turned toward Ted and smiled. Geoff stumbled and stammered for a comeback, but he held his tongue and turned his attention back to playing Solitaire on Ted's computer.

The young couple continued to crawl methodically through the questions presented to them by their Descriptive Astronomy professor. Geoff played Solitaire on the computer, occasionally stopping to make snide comments or jokes.

"God, it's ten-thirty already." Kate looked across the room at Ted's alarm clock, which clung to its perch on the wall lamp.

"Yeah. Aren't you two silly bastards done yet?" Geoff turned toward the pair, a lopsided smirk on his face.

"Geoff is it? Come here a minute." Kate opened the door and pointed at a couch in the side lobby. She held a paperback novel in her hand, which she leafed through in search of a specific passage. She stopped near the center of the book, quickly scanned the page, and gestured for Geoff to join her.

"You seem a little bored there Geoff. You like sex?"

Ted used the greatest restraint he owned to refrain from raising his hand.

"Read from where it says 'Her breasts, firm and supple, heaved beneath her cotton sweater, yearning for freedom' until the end of, well…the act. You'll know where to stop."

Geoff snatched the novel from Kate's grasp. He glanced over his shoulder at Ted as he left.

"The lobby is mine!" Geoff exclaimed in his best superhero voice.

"The park is mine!" Ted laughed in response, in a similar deep voice.

"Do what?"

"A movie we rented the other day," Ted explained. "Now, where were we?"

"Somethin' about red versus white dwarf stars." Kate sat directly beside Ted, on Geoff's sleeping bag. She slapped his left knee with her right hand, then scooped up her notebook and began to construct an answer.

* * *

The following Sunday, Ted busied himself by cleaning his dorm room. He piled a week's worth of newspapers together and stacked a dozen or so soda cans in a pyramid on the dresser. After recycling the items, he began "downsizing his files", keeping important or interesting scraps of newsprint or printed papers while discarding the others. A poster of Frank Thomas fell from the far wall, so Ted reapplied masking tape and stuck the poster to the brick surface. Darkness crept up, then took over outside as Ted worked, but he continued to clean. He stopped briefly to tend to his wounded face, scraping flaky skin from the injured area with little concern. The damage hardly existed, and Ted grinned a lopsided smirk at his reflection. His stereo blared one of his hip-hop mix tapes while he worked.

Kate walked into his room at about 8:30 PM. "Hey Ted," she deadpanned, "whatcha doin'?"

"Not much," he replied, inhaling two nostrils full of a pleasant lilac scent. He brushed beads of sweat from his brow. "Why?"

"Well, I thought you might like to head out for ice cream. I don't know, just an urge…" Kate paused for an answer.

"I'll get my coat," Ted responded, scratching the top of his head. He scooped up his black hooded pullover and slipped the garment over his head. He snatched his makeshift wallet, the photo holders from a real billfold, from the dresser. Ted kept his driver's license, student identification, bank card, and other important items in this sheath of cheap plastic with foldout windows and easily torn individual compartments. Ted flipped through the package, making sure everything he wanted was there. Snatching another pair of jeans from the floor, Ted emptied the change he found into the pants he had on. "Let's go," he muttered, breathless, swinging his key ring on his index finger.

* * *

"Hey, check this out." Kate pulled a cassette from the floorboards of her car and flipped it between her fingers. Kate's car, a tan Oldsmobile from the late 1970's, rumbled loudly toward the freeway, leaving Cheney and the campus in its rearview mirror. Kate relaxed behind the wheel, with the seat reclined at a 45 degree angle. The chair had been pulled as close to the steering column as possible to best accommodate her short legs. She grinned as she looked at the cassette tape in her fingers, then she fed it into the Oldsmobile's tape deck. "I got the 'I'm Too Sexy' single over break. But my favorite is Side B. It's got the song in Spanish. It's hilarious."

Ted leaned back farther into the plush upholstery of the passenger seat. He watched Kate's well-manicured hand slide the tape into the waiting slot. His right hand gripped the Oh Shit handle, a tactic Ted often employed when riding shotgun to redirect his nervous energy. It seemed to soothe him on longer trips when he wasn't driving.

While the stereo blasted the moronic melody, Ted stared through the windshield and out into the prairie. The royal indigo sky of early spring spread endlessly before him. A million pin pricks of light twinkled in the otherwise empty expanse of space. The prairie's surface teemed with life like a dark ocean, the tall grasses and husks of grains swaying and waving with the help of a steady breeze. A few lights glared out into the deep violet night, like buoys and lighthouses guiding weary seafarers to safety. Ted breathed in deeply, audibly, accepting all the serenity that surrounded him: the sky, the tall grass, the stars, the wind, and the beautiful woman sitting mere inches to his left, giggling silently to herself.

Kate stopped her laugh and directed her voice to Ted. "Whatcha thinkin'?"

Ted blinked his eyes. "Are these people gonna be around when we finish college?"

"Oh, um...I don't know. They're it right now, but...who knows? You know who I do think will be around a long time though?"

"Who?"

"Mr. Big. Those guys are great. You heard their album?"

"No, I haven't. Is it as good as 'To Be With You'?"

"Better. That might be the worst song on the tape."

"Really?" Ted's full attention was directed on Kate. He watched as streetlights danced over her as the Oldsmobile passed under them. The light first highlighted her elfin button nose, her large eyes, her understated lips. The light then exhibited her round chin and strong bangs for a split second. The light scanned over her shoulderlength hair, too fast to show the tans and blondes intermingled in her follicles. Finally, the artificial incandescence focused on the back of her neck, highlighting the subtle curve of the nape. Another lamp would pass by, and the image would repeat. Each cycle appeared clearer. Each repetition grew stronger. Each flash of the lamps called to Ted. "Kiss her," one whispered. "She won't mind," the next promised. "You want to," a third taunted. Ted looked forward through the windshield, shifting his attention to the approaching neon jungle of Spokane.

Kate followed the illuminated freeway into a large valley, left millennia ago by the combination of ancient glacial activity and continued erosion by the Spokane River. The city spread across the vast valley and into the surrounding hills, but at this hour the bulk of the artificial light that washed out the night sky emulated from the valley, and, more specifically, from a specific path that cut across the valley in a north-south bisection. This thoroughfare, Division Street, led north from the river cutting through the center of downtown. A person could follow this path north to a junction and conceivably be in Canada in a matter of a couple hours.

Kate exited and turned left onto Division Street. Opening the throttle, she followed the straight stretch north. With impeccable luck, Kate managed to catch every traffic light while still green. Retail business after office building, most concealed in darkness, raced by either side of the Oldsmobile. Neon decoration streamed past in a Jackson Pollock cavalcade of color.

"You know who else I like?" Kate asked. "P.M. Dawn."

"You serious? God they suck." Ted fixed his gaze on Kate once again, shifting from his intense stare out the passenger window. His contact lenses momentarily fogged, so he tried to blink them clear. He closed his left eye and tried to massage the lens with his left index finger and thumb. "I mean, their message is a bunch of hippie crap. It's all peace and love. I just can't stand it." Ted blinked quickly three more times, then was satisfied with his clearing vision.

"I like the positive stuff," Kate argued. "I know it'll make me feel better when I feel down, an' that's all right by me."

"I...guess that's fine," Ted concluded, craning his neck as a wooden shed of a bar slipped by into the darkness. "Hey, where're we goin' anyway?"

"The Safeway by my house, why?"

"Oh, nothing. It's just I have class tomorrow and can't go to Canada tonight." A wry smile crossed Ted's lips as he made the comment.

"You wish."

Ted bit his lip, struggling for a response. The best he could produce was a flagrant lie, a childish "Nuh-uh!" and he quickly cast his glance back to the passing outlines of buildings and the occasional tree.

Division forked in a Y intersection after leading down a gradual descent. Kate followed the right fork, the choice that led to the suburb of Newport. After passing an automobile dealership on the right and a small strip mall on the left, a larger shopping center loomed on the right. Kate followed the four-lane highway until she spotted the entrance to the parking lot. She directed the Oldsmobile into the lot, weaving the vehicle through a series of stop signs and white arrows. The car pulled into a parking stall in front of the last retail business in the row, the Safeway supermarket. Ted and Kate, the two close friends, both entered the supermarket at the same time.

Kate instinctively led the duo to a refrigerated bin that held frozen pizzas and individual serving sizes of ice cream. She tossed aside carton after carton of Chunky Monkey while Ted pushed aside container after container of Cherry Garcia. Eventually, Ted grew dissatisfied with the Ben and Jerry's selection and moved to the Haggen-Dazs. He tunneled toward the bottom of the cooler, when near the back left corner he unearthed the specific item he sought. Proclaiming his pleasure with a triumphant "Found it!" he victoriously pulled the container of Chocolate Chip Cookie Dough from its icy burial plot.

"Ooh!" Kate purred. "Find one a' those for me!" With that, both of them focused their search in the single open-aired cooler. Ted reached deep into the cooler with his thin arm, grasped a single cylindrical canister with his long fingers, and removed the container with a forceful tug. Success! He held the product, lid to the sky, aloft over his head for all to marvel at. Noticing only Kate and himself in the aisle, Ted sheepishly lowered his hand and gave the bounty to his companion.

They sauntered to the checkout counter and paid for their frozen treats. Kate expressed concern about utensils, but Ted reassured her that he had pilfered enough spoons from Tawanka for most of the people he knew. They piled into Kate's car and soon followed Nevada Avenue south, toward Interstate 90.

Nevada, unlike Division, was lined mostly with houses and seemed eerily dark beyond the occasional illumination from the street lamps. Hardly a stoplight impeded their steady southern progress. Before Ted knew it, the Oldsmobile passed a bar, then approached an inclining bridge. Soon, Kate followed an on-ramp toward I-90 west.

"See right here?" Ted asked, pointing at the cement guardrail barricade. Streaks of dark paint and blackened scrapes and scars decorated the otherwise drab gray surface. "That's where Maceo rubbed the rail about a week ago. I'll bet that navy streak is his."

The on-ramp pushed toward the left, then crested and began descending to the right. "See right here?" Kate remarked. "This is where Jenna killed a runaway with her Geo." Ted's stomach knotted. "The kid tried to run across in front of her. She had no time to react. They guessed he prob'ly wanted to die." Kate spoke with an even, unemotional voice, like the reporter on the evening news no doubt used when relaying the story.

"That's...that's terrible." Ted tried to picture the scene in his mind. He could imagine the accident only in slow motion. "Was Jenna okay?"

"Well, her car was pretty messed up, but she was unhurt. You know, physically. She did miss about a week of school though. I think she underwent some counseling too."

"Understandable." The image of a spindly young man in dirty clothes glaring through the windshield as he launched over the hood and headlong into the double-beamed metal guardrail haunted Ted's every thought. He tried to change the subject. "Hey, turn that up. I love this song."

Kate nudged the volume knob, then continued her trek back to Cheney. The remainder of their journey stayed quiet. Ted returned to his previous preoccupation with the beautiful opal sky, maintaining a vise grip on the Oh Shit handle. Kate kept her focus on the endless expanse in front of her. Artificial light slowly faded from view behind them; the great dark unknown stretched before them in all directions. Kate suppressed a yawn, and the two friends pushed on toward Cheney and the comfort of the dormitory.

6

June 9, 1992
What did I do wrong?

Twin elevator doors opened, and Ted wheeled his midnight black mountain bike into the lobby. He rolled the bicycle past the resident advisers' office, through a vestibule and an open pair of doors, and toward the street. There, in a parking stall along the front of the building, a white Ford Thunderbird sports coupe waited for him.

Ted rested the bike against the T-bird's quarter panel, then pulled open the rear door on the driver's side. Working deliberately, as if from a checklist, Ted snatched a powder blue bedsheet from the roof of the car and unfolded it. He carefully covered a collection of boxes and computer equipment in the back seat with the blanketing, then turned his attention to the mountain bike. Unlatching two brackets on the front fork, Ted lifted the front wheel assembly off the frame. Hoisting the frame to his shoulder, he tried to slide it into what little space remained between the pile of miscellaneous items resting on the back bench seat and the front chairs. He opened the driver's door and held down a lever, which mechanically moved the seat forward. Returning to the bike, Ted shimmied the apparatus into what little available space there was left. Ted tossed the front wheel on top of the heap, then carefully closed and locked both doors. He turned and walked toward the open entrance to the dormitory.

"Ted? Wassup?" Ted looked up to his left. Through the smoke lenses of his sunglasses, he spotted Maceo on the second floor balcony. Maceo placed a cigarette between his lips, flipped open a Zippo lighter, and inhaled until the cancer stick glowed a fiery red on its unfiltered tip. He belched a cloud of white as he continued speaking. "What's goin' on?"

"Nothin' man. I'm gettin' ready to get outta this dump." Ted leapt onto a concrete slab about three feet high. He leaned forward on his feet until his hands made contact with the side wall of the balcony Maceo occupied. Ted inched closer to the wall and rested his arms on the flat surface of this wall, crossing his arms right over left.

"Yeah, I hear you. I'm fittin' to get outta here tonight. You leavin' tonight?"

"Sorta. I'm stayin' with my dad at the hospital while he finishes his monthly shift in Spokane. Then we're going tomorrow."

"Cool." Maceo sucked on the cigarette. It glowed red as he inhaled, then went dark as he removed it from his mouth between his index and middle fingers. "So whatcha doin' this summer?"

"Not a damn thing. You?"

"Not much." Maceo billowed smoke as he talked. "I'ma find me a hella fine female, at least."

"I hear ya."

"Speaking of which, I saw your little friend around quite a lot lately."

Ted perked up at the mention of Kate. "You mean Kate?"

"Yeah. Kate. She's been making the rounds on the party scene lately." Maceo flicked ashes from his cigarette, letting the embers float over the railing to the ground below.

"I don't care," Ted replied, shifting his gaze toward the floating ashes.

"I saw her at the Delta Chi party two weeks ago, just before Memorial Day. She was pretty liquored up, dancin' with all sorts of guys. Her and her tall anorexic friend. I went up to her and said hi, but I doubt she remembers that."

"I don't care," Ted sighed.

"Then she was at the Barnburner last Thursday night, faded again. She was kickin' it with some white boy at that one. I think it mighta been your old roommate, I'm not sure."

"I don't care," Ted repeated, his chin tucked in his chest, "she can do what she wants."

"She was at the Sigma Nu house last Saturday too." Maceo took a deep drag from his cigarette.

"I don't care," Ted repeated, defensively.

"Ya know, you two are pretty close. You two should get together." Maceo took one final drag, then ground the filter into the cement with his thumb and forefinger. He then launched the butt over Ted's head to the concrete walkway below.

"We're not that close," Ted protested, standing defiant on the bulkhead. He forced his hands into the front pockets of the black-and-white checkerboard patterned shorts he wore. He paused, searching for the proper way to explain himself. "I haven't spoken to her for probably 10 or 12 days, since before Memorial Day." Maceo placed his right hip on the railing, directing his attention toward Ted and away from the ladies wandering below. "Before that, it was two weeks since I talked to her. She never went to class and wasn't around here very often. Then, the weekend before Memorial Day, I came up here Sunday night. I got to my room, where I found a note pleading for help on the Critical Thinking chapters." Ted's face began to show some color, a pale reddish hue. "I found her in the side lobby, where she told me she didn't need my help. Frankly, I haven't really missed her a whole lot since."

Ted thought for a moment, then tacked on a line. "Besides, nobody wants me anyway."

"That's bull and you know it," Maceo replied, sliding back onto his feet. "I know for a fact that one a' my friends, a female no less, said

'Maceo, your twelve-year-old looking friend is cute' and she meant you. So forget that."

"Maybe you're right Maceo," Ted said. "Hey, which friend is that anyway? You been holdin' out on a brother?"

Maceo bellowed a deep laugh, then caught his breath and said, "I don't remember who it was. It was a couple of months ago. But I do remember it distinctly."

"Speaking of forgettin' things, do you still have my Bobby Brown CD?" Ted jumped from his perch to the ground.

"I'll go get it. See ya." Maceo opened a glass door with a gentle turn and tug of the knob. Ted threw back a "Catch ya later" and entered the building.

Ted checked his room thoroughly, making sure there was nothing hiding under the beds or in the closet. He looped around the room in a counterclockwise search, checking under, inside, behind, and on top of every piece of furniture and partition in the dormitory. Satisfied with the results of his search, he backed out of the room and locked the door.

He followed his normal traffic pattern. He wandered straight down the hallway until he reached Maceo's room. Ted knocked on the door there, waited, but found no answer. The hallway veered only to the right, so Ted followed his only choice. Two rooms past Maceo's, on the left side of the brick corridor, stood Kate's dorm room. The door was open

"Ted?" A familiar voice called out as he tried to pass by in silence. He stopped and backtracked to the open portal. "You leavin' Ted?"

"Yeah. I was on my way out." Ted caught a momentary glimpse of Kate, but couldn't bring himself to keep his eyes on her. He cast his eyes to the tawny carpet.

"Before you go, could you do something for me?'

"Maybe. What is it?"

"I wanted your address so I could keep in touch with you this summer while I'm on my band tour." She reached for a day planner and began leafing through its contents, searching for an empty page.

"Why would you want to do that for?" Ted asked. As soon as the question left his lips, he lowered his head, waiting for a scolding like a toddler who had smeared finger paint on his mother's finest china.

"Let's see. Maybe 'cause your my best friend an' I wanta." She uncapped a pen, a smile on her face. Ted raised his eyes, and for the first time in nearly a month was able to look at Kate with the fondness their friendship was built upon.

What he saw took him a little by surprise. Kate's hair, normally a blonde thatch of bouncy life, seemed dull and lifeless pulled back in a tight ponytail. Her usually happy, uplifting bangs were thin and limp. Her lips looked pale, and her eyes seemed puffy and narrow. Ted knew the signs; she suffered from a lack of sleep.

"Of course," he smirked, reaching out for her day planner and pen. He inspected her hands as he reached. Her nails, or, more accurately, nubs, resembled his own fingernails. They were short, exhibiting signs of being knawed on. None of her nails were coated with fresh polish, and much of what remained exhibited cracks and other trauma. He cleared his throat, then asked, "How'd you do on that test?"

"Well, I shouldn't have missed those two weeks like I did," Kate replied. "Anyway, I told my parents not to expect too much. You?"

"Oh," Ted retorted, changing his voice to resemble their Asian professor's, "I have trouber wiss the proos." They both laughed out loud together for the first time in two months.

Ted regained his faculties and changed the subject. "So...when are you leaving?"

"I have these two boxes to put in the car an' I'm outta here."

"Well shoot, gimme one a' those since I'm leaving now too." He grabbed a sizable box, hoisting it clumsily to his chest with the help of his upper thighs. Kate grabbed the smaller box, held it under her left arm, and pulled her door shut with her free right hand.

The two best friends followed the stairs to the rear exit, then climbed a small hill and walked to Kate's waiting Oldsmobile. Kate deposited her box on the roof of her car and unlocked the passenger side door. Ted opened the door, then placed his box in the back seat. Kate followed with her box. She pushed the door closed with her hip, and she turned and faced Ted.

"Well…I'll…be…seeing you."

"Yeah Kate, um…good luck."

"Thanks. I'll talk to you soon."

"Yeah, I'll…see ya." Ted walked away from Kate's Oldsmobile as she climbed in and started the vehicle. She pulled out of the parking lot, honking at Ted and waving gleefully as she sped by him. Ted fished for his key ring, squinting in impatience as he struggled to remove the ring. Breaking his stride at the door of his parents' Thunderbird, he finally successfully retrieved the keys and unlocked the driver's side door. With a snap of the seatbelt, Ted shifted his weight to a more comfortable posture. Igniting the engine with the clockwise turn of the key, Ted put the Ford into reverse, pulled out of the parking space, and turned the wheel as he backed into the street. Soon, the Thunderbird sped out of Cheney, a white comet leaving a tan nebula behind.

Ted turned up the car stereo, then stared at his reflection in the rearview mirror. He glanced back at Cheney as it melted into the surrounding hillside of wheat and tall grass. A lot of history stayed in that town. Meanwhile, Ted's present and future spread before him in endless highways and backroads. He glanced over to his right. The chair next to him remained vacant.

Ted looked into the rearview mirror again, watching a series of tears roll down his cheeks.

7

June 29, 1992
Just when I thought it was over, it starts all over again.

Ted leaned back in a lawn chair, fidgeting for a comfortable position in the plastic and metal torture rack. His mother sat next to him, in a far less cruel piece of lawn furniture. She picked at her dark hair, scratching at an unknown itch. Mom clapped her hands together as her youngest son began a slow march toward a mesh cage.

John carried a black wooden bat on his shoulder as he adjusted his athletic supporter. He spat in the fine dirt, then kicked the dusty powder over the translucent liquid. Adjusting a blue batting helmet, John stepped into the batter's box to face Tumwater's starting pitcher. John stretched the sleeves of his powder blue West Side jersey by raising his arms over his head, swinging the black bat in a circle. The pitcher readied himself by nodding positively to the catcher. John gripped the bat menacingly, prepared to swing at the pitch.

The Tumwater 13 and 14 year-old team played its home games on an open field on Tumwater High School's campus. A diamond had been carved into the haphazardly maintained grass. A backstop built with five 15 foot high chain link panels had been hastily erected, and two plywood dugouts with green roofs and tan sides paralleled the foul lines of powdery white chalk. The right field foul territory expanded to the blacktop of a side street, while in left field bleachers ended the foul ground. The bank of bleachers faced away from the field, toward a track with a grass infield that was surrounded by a chain-link fence standing about six feet high. The facade of the bleachers read "TUMWATER" in white letters over a faded mint background. The letters were large enough and bold enough to be seen easily from Interstate 5 a tenth of a mile or so away. Beyond the facade, unseen sources created a loud melody.

"I wish they'd stop," Mrs. Jamison mumbled. Her son John fouled the first pitch behind the backstop. "You'd think they'd give up by now."

John took the next pitch low for ball one.

"Yeah. Whatever it is, they really suck at it. They keep starting over." Ted chuckled at his own comment. "Get it right!" he growled, faking anger. John let another pitch go by, low for ball two. The sound ceased, and the surroundings quieted.

John connected with the next pitch. The horsehide sphere dropped into right center field, skipping across patches of emerald grass and stretches of butterbean blades. John stepped on first base in full stride, chugging hard to second. The right fielder cut off the rolling baseball. He picked it up. He threw to the second baseman. John slid, extending his left leg toward the safety of the bag. Safe! John called for time out, then tried to brush off the combination of grass and dirt from his white baseball pants. "He can't go one game without getting dirty," John's mother commented through her clapping and the cheers and clapping of those around her, Ted included.

"Mom, I'm going to the bathroom." Ted rose from the lawn chair and found his way around the backstop. He followed the chain link fence protecting the track infield to the facade. Stopping briefly, he noticed a large group meandering around aimlessly on the grass infield. Most of them carried musical instruments: horns, trumpets, drums, and other various musical tools. He shrugged off the bizarre scene and wandered toward a nearby portable toilet.

Upon opening the synthetic door, the overwhelming stench, combined with a sweltering heat, caused Ted to frantically think of some plan to breathe. He gulped in air, then quickly closed the door and unzipped his pants. Ted began to empty his bladder, when a sudden, boneshuddering thud rattled the translucent white plastic roof of the Port-O-Let. A chorus of laughter resonated from the direction of the field, accompanied by the faint shuffle of cleats on the emerald grass. Ted realized that a foul fly ball had impacted his position. Then, like fresh urine dropping on a sneaker, the realization of the significance of the group on the track infield permeated Ted's brain.

Omigod! Kate!

He quickly finished and zipped up his jean shorts. He emerged from the Port-O-Let to cheers and clapping. Parents in chairs, players in the field, even the umpire gave him an ovation. Ted doffed an imaginary cap to the adoring crowd, then made his way along the back of the bleachers to the far end. He turned the corner and began to scan the crowd.

Young adults of all sizes milled around between the bleachers and a gymnasium, on a sidewalk under cover. A group of the young people was crowded together near the track, talking. Others disappeared into the gymnasium, sometimes returning, often not. Still more crowded around a set of tables covered with a grand spread, grabbing paper plates and filling them with fruit slices and luncheon meats. Ted spotted the target of his affection, a well-remembered length of dishwater blonde hair cascading down a narrow back. He approached and tapped Kate on her right shoulder.

She turned with startled swiftness. "Omigosh! Ted! What're you doing here?" Kate grinned widely, her eyes glistening with excitement. Ted beamed proudly in response, displaying all of his teeth.

"I live here Kate. Well, not here, but, you know, in town. Also, my brother's playing over on the field over there."

Kate chewed, then swallowed, a grape. She gulped air before speaking. "Well, this is a great surprise. How'd you know I was over here?"

"I heard the practicing and decided to come see what was going on. Then I remembered you were doin' this. I had to take a shot it was you."

"I'm glad you did. This is so great!" Kate waved at a blonde girl with thick, round glasses. "Belinda? Belinda, remember my friend Ted I told you about? This is him."

Belinda grinned slyly. "Hello," she cooed seductively, a bet-you-wish-you-knew-what-I-was-thinking tone in her greeting and gleam in her eye. Ted fired his customary "Hey" nod to her while shaking her hand with a grip like he held a wounded sparrow. He turned his attention back to Kate. "So, how long're you here for?"

"Oh, only tonight. We leave tomorrow for Sacramento. I am *not* looking forward to that bus ride at all."

"You'll be fine. It's not that far to Sacramento."

"True. But Sacramento's only our first stop. By the time we reach Wisconsin, I'll probably have gone insane."

"I'll tell you what." Ted scratched an insect bite hiding within the part of his hair. "If you start feeling loopy, go ahead and write me. I'll make sure to help snap you back to reality."

"You don't need to worry about that," Kate replied. "I planned on writing you enough so you could write me at every mail stop."

"I look forward to doing it."

A loud cheer erupted from behind Ted, in the direction of the contest between the two adolescent teams.

"Hey, best of luck. I hope to hear from you soon. I need to get back to the game now." Ted turned and stepped onto the sparse grass, headed toward the playing field.

"Ted?" Kate took a step toward him.

"Yes?"

"Thanks. It means a lot to see you. It really does."

Ted waved his hand to her, then disappeared around the corner and out of her line of sight. Belinda walked up beside her.

"Kate?" she commented, "You were right about him."

8

November 8, 1992
I've never been the luckiest man around. Lately though, things have really changed for the better. If I were old enough, I'd probably plan a trip to Vegas or something.

"Dude."
   "What?"
   "Dude."
   "What?"
   "Dude."
   "What!"
"Oh, nothing." Mark snorted an evil laugh to himself, pleased with the angry response from Ted. Mark tucked his shoulderlength jet black rocker hair behind his ear. He wore a Metallica "And Justice For All" T-shirt, which hung untucked over the waist of dark jeans. His bare feet kicked back and forth, inches from the square tiles of the floor.
"And you did that because?" Ted grumbled, turning his attention back to his latest issue of *Sports Illustrated*. He lay on his stomach, Mark to his back, his toes overlapping the foot of the bed. Contempt overwhelmed his voice.
"No reason dude," Mark cackled, a smile vanishing from his mouth.

"Then don't do it," Ted hissed.

Mark's icy stare cut into Ted. Mark quickly regained his composure, standing and shuffling to the stereo. Ted's roommate of the past two months rifled through his collection of cassette tapes, a mismatched stack of speed metal that seemed to grow daily. Mark found the tape he wanted and slipped it into the tape deck. He pushed the play button, then cut the air with a roundhouse motion of his arm, checking to make sure his air guitar was still in tune.

"Don't turn it up too loud," Ted pleaded. Mark obliged, turning the volume only to the eight setting instead of his customary full volume. Mark's whole body convulsed as he sang along with the opening cut of his selection. "Seven deadly sins…seven ways to win…seven holy paths to Hell!" Ted rolled his eyes as Mark pointed in his direction.

Just when Ted thought he would have to heave Mark off the balcony, a knock pierced the violent chords and shrill screams. Traci, five-foot-ten of platinum haired bombshell, stood in the open doorway. Though hardly possible, she looked even more gorgeous than usual. She wore a man's white shirt, the top two buttons undone to display her considerable cleavage. She completed her ensemble with tight boots and even tighter Levi's jeans.

"Turn that down," Ted insisted, motioning to Mark. Mark reluctantly fulfilled the request with a deep sigh, then mouthed a flirtatious "Hi" to Traci's chest.

"What's goin' on?" Ted asked, sliding himself into a seated position.

"A group of us are going to Kickers tonight. You guys wanna go?"

Ted weighed his options for less than a second. "Gimme five minutes to get ready." He thought for a second. "I need to sandpaper my neck to get it its reddest."

"Cute. Meet us in the elevator lobby in five minutes."

Ted pulled the only dress shirt he owned from his closet. In his new dorm room, the closet watched over the door. Actually, a closet stood on both sides. The dormitory room, normally equipped for the handicapped, had opened up over the summer and Ted found himself with the fortune of being on top of the waiting list. Unfortunately, housing officials had teamed him with Mark.

Slinging the blue cotton blend over his shoulders, Ted slid his arms through the sleeves. He buttoned the shirt, then tucked it into his blue jeans. Owning no boots, Ted slipped his black Adidas shelltoes on his feet. He quickly tousled his hair, licking his fingertips and rubbing them through his healthy brown coiffure. He turned to his roommate.

"How do I look?"

"Like a gay lumberjack."

"Thanks." He shut the door behind him, barely containing the advancing wave of electric guitar and groin shattering screeching.

Ted turned left, then, after about four steps, took a quick right followed by an even quicker left. The elevator lobby opened up before him, with its putrid orange-brown carpet and hideous modular furniture. He walked forward into the lobby and instantly was greeted by a group of four people.

Traci stood the closest to Ted. She now carried a white knit sweater, draped over her left forearm. She slid her right hand into her jeans pocket.

Cassie stood to Traci's immediate right. Cassie also wore blue jeans, which hung from her pipe cleaner legs. She sported a flannel shirt, which also hung nearly straight over her undistinguished chest. Her raven locks, curly from a recent perm, were pulled into a single berette and cascaded halfway down her back in a series of spirals. She waited patiently with her weight on her right leg, her flat ass pushed out behind her.

Sam, the only other male in the fivesome, waited in a reclined position on a couch, his feet resting on a low, square table as if it was an ottoman. He rested to Cassie's right. Sam's short, dark hair blended closely with his choice of wardrobe: black waistcoat, black jeans, and freshly shined Doc Marten boots. He wore a white T-shirt under the jacket. He rose from his seated position in Ted's presence.

Finally, Bianca stood next to Sam, impatiently grooming her fingernails. A floral print, vintage A-frame dress stretched over her overweight torso, hanging limply near her knees. White translucent stockings covered the remainder of flesh below her waist, from her knees to her Birkenstock sandals. A black bandanna held her short auburn hair away from her round face. Curled hair spread behind this hair accessory, except for bangs that had been combed forward. She flipped her fingers through the bangs, attempting to give them a fuller look.

"We should be going," Bianca complained from behind her meaty hand.

"You look nice," Cassie commented to Ted. She batted her jade eyes in his direction.

"You think so? I was worried."

"Really? 'Bout what?"

"Well, I don't own a dinner plate on a cowhide strap. Will I still fit in?" Everyone laughed when Ted made his joke.

"No, seriously," Cassie continued, "you do look nice."

"Thanks. I kinda thought I looked like a rookie truck driver."

Sam chimed in, "But without the mesh hat."

The elevator opened and the five of them filed in. They unloaded in the main lobby and made their way outside to a waiting caramel brown Ford station wagon. Bianca unlocked the doors and the group piled in. Seconds later, in a whirlwind of simulated wood paneling, the fivesome started their pilgrimage to the Washington/Idaho border.

* * *

"So, you guys all remember the 'Superfriends' right?" The words escaped Ted's lips under cover of pale near darkness, illuminated only by faint moonlight and the occasional overhead streetlight. Four heads bobbed positively; Sam shifted in the front seat so he could see Ted, who sat directly behind him. Traci and Cassie also fixed on Ted, while Bianca remained focused on the freeway before her. "Anyone want to hear my theory about that show?" Ted asked, and he was met by a silent poll of positive nods.

"Since you all remember the show, you remember the idea that the group tried to make up a cross section of races. You know, you had your white guys and a girl, Wonder Woman. But then they fought the Legion of Doom and had a bunch of other heroes. They had their black guy..."

"Ooh! Black Falcon!" Cassie interrupted.

"Yep, he's the one. Then they had an Asian, Samurai."

"I don't remember him," Traci piped up.

"He's the one who turned into a tornado when he chanted 'Nasay teehoe nee hi akoo!" Ted deepened his voice into a heroic bass. Everyone except Bianca giggled; Bianca asked for silence so she could concentrate on the road.

"Don't forget Apache Chief!" Cassie cheered.

"Yes. There was him, as well as the Mexican superhero, El Dorado. Anyway, my point is, there were superheroes representing all the minorities, most pretty blatantly. You remember the Wonder Twins right?"

"Gleek!" Cassie yelled, laughing hysterically.

"Uh huh, he was the monkey. But Jayna was the girl and Zan was the guy. Well, after careful study, I've figured out that Zan was the gay superhero."

The group remained silent. Each of them contemplated the idea. Finally, Bianca broke the silence: "That's not funny."

"It's not meant to be. It's my theory."

"Well, you're gonna have to prove it to me." Bianca's icy stare reflected back from the rearview mirror, two white spheres bathed in darkness.

"Okay, first there's the high pitched voice and the lavender jumpsuit." Ted stared back at Bianca; she blinked and cast her eyes elsewhere. "Plus, you never saw him hangin' out around anybody but guys and his sister. Whenever he teamed with someone, it was always Superman or Batman."

"Well, what about Aquaman? He could be gay," Sam wondered aloud.

"I though about that too. But he was always hangin' around with Wonder Woman, hitchin' rides in the Invisible Jet."

"What about Robin?" Sam challenged.

"You forgot about his affair with Batgirl?"

"Huh. Maybe you're right. But you know somethin'?"

"No. What?"

"You have too much time. You need a woman." The group, except for Ted, chuckled at Sam's comment.

"Oh, don't be mad." Traci consoled Ted, patting him lightly on the left leg.

"I'm not mad. I just hate it when someone shoots me down with the truth." The group quieted, and Ted shifted his eyes into the dark night sky.

After a healthy 45 minutes of traveling, the group chanced upon a structure built of logs waiting for them on the left side of a poorly lit two-lane highway. Cars and pickup trucks in tight rows lined a patch of dirt, standing a silent vigil in the parking lot. A vast field extended behind the building into the faint moonlight.

The front of the structure was lined by a covered porch. Over the porch, four foot high red neon letters announced the single building to the rest of the surrounding night. The sign read "Kickers" in script, except for the letter "I". This letter was replaced by a boot, which switched from one angle to a second position in the hum of neon gas, making it appear to everyone that the boot was kicking.

"This must be the place," Sam cracked, stating the obvious. Cassie smacked his chest with the back of her hand. Sam doubled over, faking as though he struggled in intense pain.

Ted emerged from the station wagon first. Once on firm ground, he spread his legs slightly, then slid his thumbs into two belt loops on the front of his blue jeans. Leaning back onto his heels with minute pressure, he raised his gaze with a steady pace to the bright neon sign. A lone cowboy, Ted surveyed this antique saloon on the prairie. The only thing that ruined the fantasy, other than, of course, his appearance, happened to slap him on the shoulder and return him to reality.

"Come on Ted," Bianca hissed. "Let's get this over with."

A heavy set doorman in a wide collared button-down shirt peered at the fivesome through wide rimmed glasses. One by one, each person's identification came under the careful scrutiny of the immense gatekeeper. When he finished with one driver's license, he'd hand over the laminate to its owner, then grasp the extended hand and stamp a mark on it. Sam received the number 21 on his hand, indicating that he was of legal drinking age and could purchase alcohol. The rest of the group received a star in dark indigo, a symbol of underage patronage. The group passed through without a word. Traci waited for her change, Sam made his way toward the bar, and the remaining three scanned the interior of the complex, searching for an open table.

"This'll take forever to wash off," Bianca pouted, rubbing at the back of her right hand. Cassie and Traci glanced at each other, silently daring the other to tell their heftier acquaintance to shut up. The three girls spotted an open table and started across the room, through the crowd, toward a shadowy space.

The inside of Kickers fit Ted's preconceived notions of the place almost perfectly. From the narrow corridor entering the building to the hardwood floors, it reminded Ted of every country bar he'd seen in the movies. The actual bar occupied what would be considered the front wall of the establishment. Tables and stools laid scattered about in no discernible floor pattern. Two pool tables rested near the center of the floor, guarded overhead by lamps bearing Budweiser shades. After about ten strides from the entrance, a wooden railing separated the raised gathering area from a lower dance floor. Two short steps, found in the center of the railing, aided those who wished to enter the sunken level. More square tables and armless chairs flanked either side of the dance floor, resting their legs on an olive carpet. Finally, a raised stage lined the back wall. Two electric signs reading "EXIT" framed the stage, a stage teeming with activity.

Kit and the Kickers continued through their set. Kit bellowed in a sultry voice, grasping the microphone stand with both hands while gyrating her hips. The Kickers furiously worked over their instruments. The violinist mercilessly attacked his fiddle with the bow as Sam waddled up beside Ted.

"Wassup buddy?" Sam gulped, swallowing a sip of Budweiser from a plastic cup.

"Nothin'," Ted replied, keeping his eyes glued to the curvaceous, auburn-haired firebrand in tight pants on-stage. "Just an overwhelming urge to scream 'Yeeha!'"

Sam snorted a laugh. Ted continued, "I do have one question though."

"What's that?"

"Shouldn't they have chicken wire up in front of the stage?" They both quickly chuckled.

"Nah," Sam retorted, lifting his plastic cup, "they only serve from a tap here anyway."

The girls had settled at a table, to the right of the two steps and against the railing. They waved to the guys, who acknowledged their position with twin nods. Ted and Sam worked their way through a sea of ten-gallon hats, tight jeans, and rawhide boots. They slid into chairs surrounding the table and breathed in the ambiance.

The group chatted together for awhile, through Kit and the Kickers' scheduled 20 minute break. The band resumed their brand of crowd pleasing country music cover songs, creating a steady stream of couples entering and leaving the floor. Suddenly, Ted leapt from his chair, extended his hand, and grumbled a quick "Come on" to Traci. She grasped his outstretched palm before she had the chance to protest, and the two of them bounded down the steps and onto the dance floor.

Ted and Traci spun and twirled, at times looking like they knew the steps they attempted. Ted swung Traci out wide, then passed her behind him. Switching hands while making the pass, Ted extended her wide again, then pulled her back in close to him. He followed up by spinning her and making a sloppy exchange to again hold both her hands. They continued trying steps and spins, moves and switches, throughout the song. Laughing, they left the floor to raucous applause from their compatriots. Traci gave Ted a hug, using her arms but keeping her body at a safe distance.

Time dragged along slowly, but the eerie feeling that time sped by came in the same instance. The group chatted and laughed. The five friends kept returning to the subject of Ted's roommate Mark. None of them could solve the mystery of how two completely different individuals were thrown together. "I think the dorm director must have smoked too much crack that day" was Ted's only explanation. Ted sipped a Coca-Cola, then stopped midstream and diverted his attention from the caramel colored beverage to the dance floor.

Individuals stepped into rows on the hardwood surface. Each person completed a series of steps, then dipped a shoulder forward. They continued moving, then made a distinctive crossover step that set Ted into a frenzy of excitement.

"That's the Electric Slide!" Ted shouted. "That's ghetto!"

"So?" Bianca snarled, raising her heavy head from her cupped right hand.

"I can do ghetto!" Ted proclaimed proudly. He rose to his feet.

"So get down there," Cassie urged Ted, pushing a midnight strand of curly hair from her eyes.

Ted jumped down the stairs and found his rhythm as he found a spot amongst the throng. He stepped in time with everyone else on the floor, grinding his hips when they ground theirs, dipping when they dipped. Ted's smile beamed widely as he moved with the crowd. He caught a glimpse of his companions, who cheered when he flashed a thumbs up to them. The step required everyone to turn left, which Ted knew well. When he made the step, he looked to his left. His wide grin vanished.

A dark silhouette danced next to him, making the same moves he made. Even concealed in shadow, this figure seemed familiar. The shape of the body appeared very similar to one Ted knew well in his mind. But it couldn't be! He refocused his attention on the dip and crossover step, then the turn to the left.

The figure stood directly in front of him. From his vantage point, Ted studied the mysterious female, head to toe. The hair, shorter and thinned considerably, still showed its bouncy life. The narrow shoulders still emptied into a slim back. The hips still were supported by short legs. Ted knew this frame quite well. It's hard to forget what your best friend looks like.

The crowd stepped left again, and Ted confirmed Kate's presence. Light bathed her body with brilliance. Ted's hands grew clammy as he looked at her button nose. His breathing became forced as he wandered down her body with his wide eyes. His heart skipped faster as she performed a quick grind of her hips. Ted followed along as best he could, but his steps now came halfheartedly. He stayed on beat, but he no longer displayed the same type of enthusiasm he showed just seconds before. The Kickers came to the end of the song, finishing with a forceful gesture by the guitarist, who knifed the air with his instrument. The crowd, both on the dance floor and in the raised area, clapped their approval. Kate exited the floor, heading to a table to the right of the dance floor. She took a seat next to a taller blonde girl in glasses.

Ted circled behind one table, concealing himself in shadows, then crept up on Kate. He clasped her shoulder with his left hand. She instinctively yanked her shoulder away, spinning her head to face her unknown assailant.

"Ted?" she gasped, half out of breath, half in shock. She quickly recovered. "What're you doin' here?"

"I came with some friends," Ted explained. He turned and pointed in their direction, not far from Kate's position. The ladies waved a hand; Sam lifted his plastic cup in tribute. "How 'bout you?"

"I'm here with Belinda," Kate replied. She nodded toward her companion. "You remember Ted, don't you?" Belinda returned a nod, then flashed a smile at Ted.

Ted tried to change Kate's focus, sitting in a chair next to her. "So, whatcha been up to lately? I haven't heard from you."

"Not much. Just school." Kate's eyes darted around the room. Failing to find anything more interesting, Kate's eyes fell once more on Ted. "Oh, and band."

"Yeah. How's that goin'?"

"Good. At least we don't have to travel when the football team leaves town." She squeezed her right hand into a fist, holding for a few seconds before releasing the clench. "How about you?"

Ted ran his left hand through his hair, past his left ear. "Classes are fine so far. I'm gettin' along well with most of the people on my floor. I hate my new roommate though."

"Why's that?"

"He's a rocker," Ted said matter-of-factly. Kate nodded in agreement.

Ted thought for another angle to choose, rubbing his chin. He turned slightly in his chair until he faced both Kate and Belinda. "So, tell me about the T-shirts you two bought in Wisconsin."

Kate chuckled, knowing what Ted referred to. "Oh, you mean Saddam Condoms..."

"For dicks who refuse to pull out." Belinda finished Kate's sentence for her. The two of them laughed loudly. Ted smiled gleefully, soaking in Kate's bright face.

Bianca caught Ted's attention in the corner of his eye, pointing repeatedly and violently at her bare wrist, at an imaginary watch. "Kate, I gotta go," Ted apologized. "Maybe I'll call you sometime."

"Sure. That would be great."

"Belinda, it's good to see you again. You two have fun this evening." Ted turned and bounced up the steps, joining Cassie, Traci, Bianca, and Sam on the landing. The group filed toward the exit. Ted stopped, turned back toward the stage, and breathed in deeply as he took one last glance at his best friend. He built a mental picture of her golden silk hair and smooth cewpie doll skin, a lasting image of her perfect, tiny frame.

Belinda leaned forward and said to Kate, in a low voice, "He's checkin' you out."

"I know."

9

January 23, 1993
For the first time in my life, I think I'm thinking clearly.

A hollow knock echoed off the door. Ted hurriedly pulled on a pair of black shorts, then kicked a damp towel and a pile of clothes into the closet as he passed. He grabbed the cold steel door knob and turned it to the right. The latch gave way, and he pulled open the gateway to find Kate standing in the hallway.

Ted's brow rose in surprise. "Hey!" he exclaimed happily. "How are you?"

"Fine." Kate beat water from her white windbreaker with her gloved hands.

"Well, come in." Ted held the door open for his best friend, who sauntered by him. She removed her heavy ski gloves, placing them on top of the dresser. She unzipped the windbreaker, then lifted the jacket over her head and slipped her arms free. Droplets of water pooled together on the tiles of the floor, sliding from the garment that rested draped over the back of a desk chair. She glanced to her right.

"What happened to the other bed?" Her back was turned to Ted. Kate focused her attention on the empty corner where Mark's bed once sat.

"Mark finally got fed up and moved out," Ted explained, combing his wet hair into place with a brush. "I took the two mattresses and stacked them on one frame. I put the other frame in storage." Satisfied with his hair, Ted stepped to the door, pushing it softly and listening to the deadbolt click into place.

"Not a bad idea." Kate turned to face Ted. "I, uh, have an hour before my next class. I was wondering if I could…stay here until then?" She cocked her head to the side, waiting for Ted's response.

"Not a problem." Ted grabbed the short collar of the gray sweatshirt that covered his torso and tugged forward. With a quick adjustment, he found the spot where the garment fell true about his neck and released his grasp. Ted turned his attention to the desk behind Kate, lifting a purple spiral notebook from the bone colored plastic counter. He sat on his unmade bed and leafed through a thick textbook, which lay propped open on top of a stack of two flat pillows. Stopping at a specific passage, he turned to the notebook and cross-referenced the selected poem with his notes from the lecture about the piece.

Kate pounced on the bed, sending a wave and a cool gust across the surface of the mattress and through tiny canyons in the folds of the comforter. She settled next to Ted. Their hips touched lightly, her right and his left. Ted felt the soft cotton of her sweater sleeve brush across his bare flesh as excess material that hung from her elbow passed over his exposed left leg. She moved hair from her face, tucking the maize strands behind her ear as she fixed her eyes on the notes sitting in Ted's lap. "So, what's this?"

"Oh, it's a…a paper I need to finish. I'm supposed to use examples from the text to, uh, describe the concept of unrequited love."

"Unrequited love." Kate repeated the phrase slowly.

"Yeah. I'm using the despair of the narrator in T.S.Eliot's 'Love Song of J. Alfred Prufrock' as the basis for my argument. You see, I'm proving that love unfulfilled is worse than never knowing the person. The wondering…what might have been…can be unbearable." Ted tapped a Bic on the notebook.

"Really? I've always believed in the idea of it's better to have loved and lost than to run from the rejection." Kate paused, scratching the outside of her nose. "That's a tough one."

"Here. Listen to this." Ted scanned a page in his text, then stopped when he found the passage he wanted.

> "And indeed there will be time
> To wonder, 'Do I care?' and, 'Do I dare?'
> Time to turn back and descend the stair,
> With a bald spot in the middle of my hair—
> (They will say: 'How his hair is growing thin!')
> My morning coat, my collar mounting firmly to the chin,
> My necktie rich and modest, but arrested by a simple pin—
> (They will say: 'But how his arms and legs are thin!')
> Do I dare
> Disturb the universe?
> In a minute there is time
> For decisions and revisions which a minute will reverse."

Ted stopped for a second, swallowing. "As you can see, he's worried about what's happening to him. He doesn't like the thought of being rejected."

"That's…sad," Kate responded, forlorn. "And yet…it's…beautiful."

"Kate?"

"Yes?"

"It's no more beautiful than you are." Ted leaned over toward Kate. He dropped the pen to the floor, then raised the empty hand and lightly lifted Kate's chin. Resting the hand on her cheek, Ted moved forward with his shaking lips. He closed his eyes as he approached, then softly pressed his lips against hers. After a matter of seconds, but what felt like days, Ted jerked back violently.

"Oh my God!" he ejaculated. "I'm—I...What did I...Wha—I..."

"Ted?"

"I'm...I uh..."

"Ted!"

"Hunh?"

"Shut up." Kate jumped from her seated position into Ted's arms. He tried to hold her up, but her momentum pushed him over. His shoulders crashed against the wall. Kate pushed her mouth flush with his. Ted's eyes widened in amazement, a shock that, combined with Kate's tongue, snatched the wind from his lungs. His left shoulder and upper arm managed to catch the power cord attached to the alarm clock, which sat perched on a lamp that was screwed into the wall. The alarm clock teetered, then slipped from its lofty precipice. Ted caught the appliance with his left hand and laid it gently beside him, never once relinquishing the connection he maintained with Kate's lips. He moved the free left arm to Kate's back, squeezing her closer. His hand gripped her shoulder. A thin strap rested under Kate's sweater, off her shoulder and pinned in Ted's grip. Ted rolled Kate toward the wall. A flat pillow spilled to the floor, the English textbook riding on its back. Ted pulled Kate still closer to him, continuing to explore his pent-up affections with her open mouth.

Suddenly, Ted heard a key entering the door knob, a faint scrape of metal on metal. A click followed, then a low squeak. A rush of air sliced through the room. At the same time, Ted noticed a loud, constant electronic whine originating from the hallway.

"Ted? Ted? Come on!"

Ted lifted up on his palms, pushing himself into a seated position.

"Ted! Fire alarm! Let's go!" The third floor resident adviser's voice overshadowed the scream of the fire alarm. Ted grumbled a response and stumbled from his blue sheets to a standing position. He clawed his way through the darkness, groping for his jacket. He slipped the heavy red coat over his shoulders, then wandered into the light. Without his contact lenses, Ted could make out shapes and colors but not much else. He stumbled sleepily down the hallway, in a daze, squinting to find his way better. Reaching the stairwell, Ted immediately encountered a fuzzy throng of blurry faces and sketchy bodies.

The cold slapped his face when he reached the outside of the building. He could make out a field of eggshell white mounds in the darkness, a darkness broken in places by overhead street lamps. Faces that might be familiar under normal circumstances were shadowy, surreal smears of color and faint shapes. Ted narrowed his eyes, able to make out that many of those in attendance wore pajamas or flannel sleeping garments. Many of the people in the crowd wore slippers or thongs. One girl sported a towel wrapped around her head like a turban. Very few of the people around Ted were dressed for the elements. Ted then realized that his legs felt very cold.

Ted looked down and noticed, for the first time, that his clothes ended about three inches above his knees. In his extreme haste to vacate the towering inferno, Ted neglected to find his sweatpants. He grabbed his winter jacket, but didn't get any pants, or, for that matter, any footwear. To complicate matters, Ted stood barefoot directly in the center of a wet, icy floor mat.

Ted scanned the area around him, then settled on a nearby concrete and brick windowsill. He tucked his quivering wheat chaff legs into his jacket as best he could; meanwhile, he turned his back to a steady cold breeze. Two howls, one the wind, the other the fire alarm, were drowned out mercifully by familiar voices.

"Hey Ted," Bianca muttered through chattering teeth. Bianca and her boyfriend, Dirk, huddled tightly together. Dirk appeared to wear a dark coat, likely his leather jacket. Bianca carried a large rectangle of multiple colors across her shoulders. They both smelled of a combination of cigarettes and sex.

"Hey."

"You look miserable." Dirk snorted as he made his observation, peering through his long bangs.

"I'm a little cold, but I'll be alright."

"Hey! Ted!" Sam wandered up the hill to the group, climbing the slope on the back side of the building. His entire body, from his torso covered in a leather jacket to his feet covered in Doc Marten boots, carried a distinctively dark look. Obviously, Sam had just returned from one of his frequent late night adventures.

"Hey Sam. Where ya been?" Ted lifted his chin from his chest and craned his neck to catch a scratchy glimpse of Sam.

"Oh you know me. Out." Sam removed a thin shaft of white from a palm sized white rectangle with a red lid. Dirk produced what was presumably a lighter, flicking the device and creating a high teardrop of orange flickering light. Sam sucked deeply, making sure to produce a faint red glow on the end of the emphysema rod. He exhaled a plume of smoke from his lungs. "Why aren't you gone? It is a long weekend."

Ted responded quickly to Sam's query. "I know that. Thing is, I got Sonics tickets in two weeks. I'll go home then."

"Well, looks like a few of us got stuck here M.L.K. weekend." Sam took another deep drag, then let wispy smoke escape through his mouth. "What should we do?"

"Party?" Ted, Dirk, and Bianca all answered in unison.

Sam paused for a moment, for dramatic effect. "I concur." He smiled wryly. The low howl of the fire alarm ceased. "Who else is here?"

Bianca took a quick inventory. "Traci went home for the weekend. Cassie, she's here. I think Maceo stuck around. I don't know about anybody else."

"Okay," Ted said, "sounds good. Sam, come by tomorrow and get some beer money from me."

"Ted, you always pay."

"Hey. It's only money." Teresa, the same resident adviser who saved Ted from certain death, pushed open the door and let the coeds return to the warmth of the brick bunker. The large group of students filed in, a huddled kaleidoscope of tired mass. Ted and his friends remained outdoors, waiting for the other students to disperse. Once the crowd died down, the four friends reentered the building, climbed the stairs to the third floor, and returned to their respective rooms.

* * *

Sam tossed Ted a full bottle of Peppermint Schnapps. Ted already held a 40 ounce of Olde English malt liquor between his legs, rested on his left inner thigh. Ted twisted open the cap, slipping the bottle of peppermint liquor underneath the polyester blend fabric of his St. Louis Blues hockey sweater to loosen the lid. He leaned back on the bed until his back rested against the bricks. He splashed the alcohol on his tongue, then swallowed the liquid. A warm trail descended from his throat to his digestive tract. "Whoa!" he remarked, an amazed giggle in his voice. "It's like mouthwash! Cool!" He accepted a larger swig, swishing it around inside his mouth before swallowing.

"I can't stay long. Derek might call." Cassie sipped from a can of Miller Lite. She carefully poured a small sip of beer into her mouth, leaning forward to ensure that no alcohol got on her clothes. She wore a short sleeved shirt with a cavalcade of vertical stripes, a series of reds, purples, yellows, greens, and blacks. The shirt was tucked into the waist of faded blue jeans. She sat on the bed next to Ted, close but at a safe distance.

"Oh, come on now," Ted scolded. "Put the phone in the hall or something." Cassie backhanded him, a short-armed open hand to the shoulder.

Maceo cracked open a bottle of Heineken, prying off the cap with a plastic opener attached to his key ring. He returned his keys to a pocket on the outside of a red pullover jacket, which lay sprawled over the back of the chair he reclined in. Maceo lifted the green tinted glass bottle to his lips with his left arm, at the same time picking exposed foam padding from the arm rest with his right hand. High socks and low, baggy shorts combined to allow only about three inches of caramel skin to show, a pair of ashy knees. Maceo moved his right arm, pulling on the left sleeve of his gray hooded sweatshirt with the appendage. Settling deeper into the chair, he sipped the bottle of Heineken.

Sam gulped down a mouthful from his own bottle of Heineken. His flannel shirt, left completely unbuttoned, revealed a concert T-shirt for a band called the Misfits, a maniacally grinning white face on a black background. A long fob chain hung loosely from his front pocket, connected to a belt loop. He flipped a couple links of the thin rope chain in his fingers, accidentally removing his leather wallet from his pocket in the process. The rawhide billfold flopped lifelessly to the floor. "Smoke break?" Sam asked the room, stooping in his chair to collect the misplaced wallet. He shoved the pouch back into his pocket, then snatched a Zippo lighter, decorated with the logo of the United States Marine Corps, from the top of the dresser.

"I'll join you." Dirk rose to his feet. He patted the exterior of his leather jacket until he uncovered the desired pocket and retrieved a hard pack of Marlboros. A snap of his wrist, and two cigarettes poked their scrawny tobacco necks through a hole left in the protective seal on top of the box. Placing the former between his own lips, Dirk handed Sam the latter. Sam led the way out the door, followed closely by Dirk, who clip, clap, clip, clapped his way along in worn Birkenstocks.

The door creaked shut, helped by Bianca's gentle nudge with her outstretched left arm. She shifted her weight with a slide toward the center of the second dorm bed, depositing herself directly across from the position shared by Cassie and Ted. Like Sam, Bianca also wore an unbuttoned flannel logger's shirt. Olive leggings covered her thick legs. Like Dirk, she wore Birkenstocks, but hers were newer; the cork soles hadn't broken through yet. She inspected her fake fingernails, and, satisfied, grabbed a can of Miller Lite.

Ted continued a steady drain of schnapps into his system from the glass flask. "Here, have some," he offered Cassie, who shrugged off his advance. Undaunted, he handed the bottle toward Maceo. Maceo graciously accepted the offer, extending his butterscotch hand and grasping the bottle by its neck. Unscrewing the lid, he tipped the container to his lips. Maceo nodded his approval, then returned the bottle to Ted.

Ted pushed the left sleeve of his hockey jersey to his elbow. He worked with the sewn cuff, sliding the stitching above his left elbow to keep it held fast there. All material below the first yellow band disappeared, bunched together like a Water Wing on his bicep. He repeated the task with the right sleeve, then uncapped his peppermint liquor. He brushed his right thumb and forefinger across the rim of the bottle, then tilted his head back and accepted more alcohol into his throat. "I'm fittin' to get hella drunk!" he announced to a chorus of giggles from his compadres.

Dirk entered the room to a mad shuffle of hands. Sam followed, but he stopped in the doorway. "Cassie?" Sam's voice sounded forced. "I think your phone's ringing."

"Derek!" She sprinted, instantly in full stride from her seated position, beer can in hand. She charged into Sam, then bounced off his hefty upper torso. Cassie pirouetted on her left foot, torquing on her knee, then spun and reached her door. She kicked the door while turning the knob and pushing, nearly falling to her knees when the door gave way. She disappeared into her strangely quiet dorm room.

Sam grinned widely from his stance in the doorway. "Of course, I was outside. Coulda been from anywhere."

"Bastard!" The word reverberated around the corner, followed by a hollow, heavy slam. Cassie reentered Sam's room in a huff, wedging her slim frame between Sam and the doorjamb. She stood in the center of the room, flashing Sam her middle finger.

"Seriously though," he replied, "I do have a question for you. I've already asked everyone else here."

"And what might that be?"

"What color are your nipples? Are they pink, or are they brown?"

"What?!?"

"No, see...it's not bad, really. I can prove a point just by asking the one question. I've already proved it with everyone else."

"You...did?" Cassie placed her hands on her hips in disbelief while flashing a quick glance at the other four faces surrounding her.

"Yeah," Ted responded, "mine are brown."

"Brown for me," added Maceo.

"Pink," Bianca continued.

"And pink," Dirk finished.

"Hmm...I...think they're...pink. No, wait...yeah. No...oh dammit, I'll be back." Cassie started for the door. Sam, ever the showman, held the door for her and extended his left arm, palm outstretched, toward the nearby restroom entrance. Cassie flashed an evil scowl as she passed him, then threw open the bathroom door, a growl in her throat.

"So...what can you prove?" Bianca leaned forward, her eyebrows raised.

"That she's the easiest one here to mess with."

Everyone erupted into a fit of laughter. Maceo doubled over in his chair; Ted fell to his side on the bed, his face buried in the blankets. A "not funny" echoed through the restroom. Ted lifted back to a seated position. He snorted uncontrollably, then spilled schnapps from his mouth.

Dirk chuckled and pointed at Ted's wet chin. "Whoa, party foul, dude." Ted ran the back of his hand over his chin, removing the damp area.

"You know the rule," Sam instructed. "That's a two shot foul. So set 'em up and knock 'em down."

Ted shook the bottle of schnapps. The remaining clear liquid sloshed in the bottom quarter of the flask. "Will this do?" he asked, getting a positive nod from Sam in response. Tilting his head back, Ted spilled the remaining liquor into the back of his throat, finishing off the bottle with a forced gulp and a grin.

* * *

"Come on Dirk," Sam pleaded, "either win or lose, but do something." Dirk played an eight of clubs, then inched forward. Sam followed Dirk's play by dealing an eight of hearts from his deck. Five hands clashed together over the discard pile. The hands lifted, revealing Sam's palm on the bottom of the pile. He picked up the stack of cards, adding them to what he already possessed. Maceo shook his wrist, then rubbed the injured area with his left hand.

Egyptian Ratscrew carried simple rules, making it a favorite pastime for both the drunken and the sober. Each player would play a card on a pile. When a face card or ace emerged, the next player clockwise needed to play a face card or the dealer of the face card earned the right to add the discard pile to his collection. A player needed to find a face card within four cards if an ace was played, three for a king, two for a queen, and in one card if a jack showed his face. Whenever consecutive cards carried the same value, like the pair of eights, all the players would slap for the discard pile. Whoever slapped first, the hand on the bottom, received the discards. Even a player who didn't start with any cards could slap in and eventually win the game, gaining the entire deck of cards.

The group of six sat in the side lobby. Sam and Dirk held all the cards between them. Bianca stood with her back to the bricks. The three others hovered around the table, their palms ready to pounce on any doubles.

Sam slapped down an ace. "Crap!" Dirk exclaimed in disappointment. He flipped over the four of clubs, then slapped the pile. Knowing he owed a two card penalty for slapping when doubles were not present, Dirk turned over his two remaining non-face cards. "You're Ratscrewed!" Ted remarked, ducking into his nearby room with a pronounced stagger.

"Smoke?" Sam asked the group, sliding the deck of cards to the center of the table. Maceo stood up, retracting matches from his coat pocket.

"I'll join you!" Ted yelled. He appeared in the doorway of his room. He had a brown paper bag dipped toward a deep plastic cup. A copper liquid poured from the paper sack into the beverage container.

"Would you take that bottle outta the bag already?" Bianca snarled.

"Nope. This is gangsta beer, an' I'ma gonna drink it the gangsta way." Ted stumbled momentarily, disappearing once more into the sanctity of his room.

Cassie leapt over the back of the couch, skidding her heel over the modular surface. "I'm callin' Derek," she announced, then she disappeared into her room.

"C'mon Dirk," Bianca ordered, extending her left hand. Dirk reluctantly stepped to her side, softly kissing her cheek.

Sam looked across the room at them; meanwhile, Ted emerged from his room, cup in hand. Sam asked, "Where're you two going?"

"C'mon now Samwell, you know." Ted sipped from his cup, swaying slightly on rubbery legs. "They're going to have…" he stopped, raising his chin minutely, "…the sex." He nodded his head down to emphasize the words.

"Ah yes," Sam agreed, "The coitus."

Maceo joined in. "Oh, the Happy Fun Game."

"Rrrrumpay Bumpay." Ted swallowed Olde English, walking past the couple with a wobbly staggering strut and toward the door to the balcony. Bianca cast a dirty scowl over the room; Dirk pumped his fist about belt high. The duo disappeared down the corridor.

Sam held open the door for Ted. Maceo already puffed freely on a cigarette, a halo of smoke rising above him into the crisp night air. Ted planted his buttocks on the concrete wall, the small of his back resting against a metal railing. Sam backed into a far corner, lighting his Marlboro with a match.

"Ya know what?" Ted pondered to the night. "Gimme one a' those." He pointed to Sam's cigarette, resting between his forefinger and ring finger near his left hip.

"You...sure?" Sam's mouth hung agape for a moment. Meanwhile, his right hand entered a coat pocket, emerging with a hard pack. He slapped the carton's bottom. A fresh, white sleeve of tobacco popped its head through the hole. Sam held out the pack to Ted, who carefully removed the cigarette from the package with an unsteady, shaky hand. A timid "I'm sure" slid from his liquor soaked lips.

He nestled the cigarette gingerly into the corner of his mouth. Sam tossed him a matchbook while Maceo fished for his lighter. Ted struck a match, which immediately died.

"Turn your back to the wind when you light it," Maceo instructed, "and cup the thing with your hand."

Ted followed the instructions, staggering around 180 degrees. He again struck a match, quickly raising the fragile flicker to the end of the cigarette. Once again, nothing.

"You done this before?" Maceo chuckled.

Ted struck a third match. "Sure," he replied from the corner of his mouth. He lifted the match, forming a tight protective pocket around the precious fire with his free right hand. Sucking air in frantically, he worked quickly to light the pole of rich tobacco flavor. The cigarette's tip lit up the palm of Ted's cupped hand with a dim crimson glow. Success! He inhaled a deep breath. Suddenly, hot smoke poured down his esophagus into his lungs for the first time. Ted coughed, gagged, gasped for air. Through the intense burning, Ted coughed "Haven't!" as his head began to swim. Sam and Maceo giggled, then Sam flashed a series of hand signals to Maceo.

"Hey! What's that?" Ted reclaimed his breath. He tightened his grip on the metal railing. No matter how hard he concentrated, he couldn't get Sam to stop moving in a clockwise ellipse. Actually, the whole world around him moved that way, spinning high and then low. He pointed to Sam's hands. "Show me that."

"It's sign language. I'll take it slow." Sam pointed at Ted's chest. "You."

"Are." Sam formed a symbol with his fingers, the sign for the letter R.

"One." He pointed to the air with his index finger.

"Big." Sam spread his arms, palms up.

"Time." His next sign was to point to his wrist, like he wore a watch. Sam stopped gyrating in place, and Ted's tunnel vision began to blink away as he puffed from his cigarette. Ted's body caught up to the effects of the cancer rod. Instead of being heavily intoxicated and dangerously uneasy on nicotine, he now only showed the aftermath of a strong drinking binge enhanced by a smoke break.

Sam pointed to the sky with his index finger and extended his thumb straight out. His palm looked toward Ted. The thumb and forefinger formed what appeared to be a capital L. Sam took the symbol and slapped it off his own forehead. With emphasis, Sam remarked, "Loser."

"Nice." Ted puffed heartily at his cigarette. The three of them belched smoke, three wispy ghosts that rose and dissipated into the crisp, dark night.

Ted had inhaled his cigarette nearly to the filter when Cassie stepped out onto the balcony and into the darkness and shadows. She stopped dead in her tracks at the sight of Ted, a droopy eyed mess with a bead of red glowing from the corner of his mouth.

"You're smoking!" she exclaimed. Her lower jaw hung so low in shock it seemed as though it had unhinged from her skull.

"Omigod!" Ted shouted in disbelief, pulling the spent filter from his lips. "How'd that get there?" Ted flicked the filter to the ground, then disposed of it under his heel. Sam and Maceo laughed together heartily.

"Why are you doing that?" Cassie pleaded. She raised her arms toward her head, and, in doing so, brushed Ted's cup of Olde English. The cup teetered, then gave in to inertia and toppled over the ledge. Ted lunged and pinned the cup against the concrete wall with a drunken hand. His heroic move could not save the liquid gold, which fell to the sidewalk below in a heartwrenching, wet crash. The four drinking buddies began to chuckle, then Sam silenced the group with a finger pressed to his lips.

"We probably woke up the dorm director. We should go inside before he sends someone up here to stop the underage drinking."

The group filed back into the side lobby in a silent single file line. Ted carried his empty cup, using his left arm to keep the wall off his face as he stumbled toward his room. Cassie led the group; she veered to the right, then unlocked her door and closed it tightly behind her. Maceo mumbled something about his friends across the building having a party of their own, then disappeared around the corner on his way to the elevator lobby. Sam stopped at a square table in the side lobby, stooping over to collect his deck of playing cards. Ted reached his room, pushed through the unlocked door, and retrieved a half gone bottle of Olde English from the closet to the right of the door.

* * *

Sipping the final few precious drops of malt liquor from the bottle, Ted turned his head to greet a presence that entered his room. "Whatup Sam?"

"Wassup Ted?"

"My blood alcohol content."

"I bet." Sam walked across the room, choosing to take a seat at the foot of Ted's bed. Ted flipped pages of a notebook with his fingers. He found the cover and folded it over to the outside, then opened a nearby drawer and dropped the notes in, green cover down. Sam noticed the notebook, and asked, "What's that?"

"Ah, just some old notes." Ted used his weight to slide around to face Sam. "So what's goin' on?"

"Well Ted, I must say I'm surprised. When I first met you, I thought you were all high and mighty and stuff, not wanting to waste your time with the likes of me. But now…that I know ya…you're a cool guy."

"Thanks man. I appreciate that coming from you."

"So here's my question. Why aren't you dating?"

"Wha?" Ted's eyes, droopy partially because of drowsiness but mostly from beer, widened a little. He leaned forward, intrigued by the conversation.

"I get it. Girl at home huh?"

"No…there's nothing for me there in any way, shape, or form."

Sam leaned closer. "Then…what is it? Don't like women?"

"Nah, hell no. I think women are great." Ted crossed his arms and settled deeper into the chair.

"See, the way I see it, you're great. You treat people right. You're intelligent, funny, a good sense of humor. Cassie seems to really dig you."

Ted shifted his weight at that comment. "But she has that Derek guy. I don't do that, breakin' people up."

"See? You're also classy, don't play games. God, I can think of a dozen women right now who need a guy like you."

Ted uncrossed his arms and began to scratch at lime green material with his right index and middle fingers. He sighed, then responded. "The problem is, I'm not sure I believe that. Besides…" He rubbed his left eye, then ran the hand by his left ear.

"What?"

"There's only one girl I want."

Sam leaned back a moment, then stood up and moved to Ted's second chair. He acclimated himself with the flat padding and unforgiving back, then retorted. "Now we're gettin' somewhere. So…who is she?"

"Her name's Kate," Ted quickly spouted. "Maceo knows her. She lived on this floor last year when I did. Oh, you know, she's the one I talked to at Kickers that night." Ted looked for a positive response of recognition from Sam, but got only a blank stare. Ted's left leg began to shake.

"Uh huh. This is great. So you like her?"

"How could I not? When I came here, I expected to just float. You know, I'd do my four years, leave with a degree, nothin' else. Then she came along and all the other stuff became...important." Ted sniffed air through his dry sinuses, then breathed out heavily. "She's the best friend I ever had..."

"And you're afraid to lose that."

"Yuhuh." Ted sniffed again. "You'd love her Sam. Everything about her is so...beautiful. She has this great hair like spun gold. Her eyes, they light up the darkest day with blue happiness. God...everything about her...wonderful. She even has nice elbows. How often do you hear that? But she does." Ted scratched his right forearm, pushed up his falling sleeve. "Even so, it's her personality that is best."

"How so?"

Ted ran both hands through his hair. Both his legs vibrated nervously in place. "You see, after my granpa died, I went through a...tough time. I was a burden to be around. My friends left me...they wanted to have fun. For Godsakes! It was high school!" Ted rubbed moisture from beneath his nose. "That's kinda why I'm here; I wanted out of my situation." Ted paused, wiping the corner of his right eye with his right thumb. "For two years, I wasn't happy more than two days in a row. I couldn't be. I didn't remember how. Then she came along, and I learned how again. I mean, when I felt bad, when I felt good, whenever, when I saw her, when I see her, it lifts me up that much more. *That's* why she's my best friend, the best I ever had." He sighed deeply once, twice. He shook in his seated position.

"So do you love her?"

"Man I don't throw that word around lightly. I hate when people say 'I love my car' or 'I love that song' or things like that, throwing such a strong, important emotion into something so trivial. I'm not sure what love is supposed to be like, but I sure as hell hope it's exactly like how I feel for Kate. So yeah...I...think I do." Ted breathed hard, letting the air out in a forceful push. His eyes stung, felt warm and moist. "You know what sucks most of all?"

Sam started to ask, but Ted cut him off. "I can't tell if she feels the same way." His eyes swelled full with salty water. "I mean, she's my *best friend*. I can't lose that." A streamlet rolled down his right cheek. He sniffed in a wet sniffle.

"I know it hurts man. But sometimes you gotta go for it. It's easy to say 'hi'; saying 'I love you' is the hard part."

Ted brushed a tear from his left cheek, took a heavy breath, and continued. "I know. But if I told her, and she didn't feel the same way, I don't…know if…I could handle it. And if she left me…" he sobbed gently, "left me behind…never spoke to me…I'd…I'd…die." Ted covered his face with both hands. Torrents of tears rushed from his eyes. He forced air in and out of his lungs, whimpering softly each time he tried to exhale.

"She'd never do that," Sam quietly reassured Ted. "Now, I don't know her, but if she's anything like you say…anything close…even if she doesn't feel the same way she'll still be your friend. She won't shut you out."

Ted raised his stinging eyes from his hands. He brushed tears from his cheeks, then stained his shorts with his wet palms. He slowly took a deep breath; his sobbing subsided. "You know what I'm gonna do?" he asked, then answered his own question. "Her birthday's on the twentieth, and I'm thinkin' of sending her some roses."

"That's a very good idea, Ted. I really think she'll like that."

Ted grinned weakly. He tasted a salty drop on his tongue, lapping it from his upper lip. "Yeah…yeah, that'll be good. She'll really like that. Sam, thanks for listenin'."

"Anytime big guy. I'm gonna get up outta here. You gonna be okay?"

"Oh yeah, sure. Already am."

"Good. Just remember, keep the faith buddy." Sam rose to his feet and left the room. Ted walked to the dresser, then stared into the mirror as he gathered his toothbrush, toothpaste, and contact lens items. He peered at his swollen, bloodshot eyes, his puffy pink cheeks.

Everything's gonna be all right. This will work out for the best.

* * *

The heavy door resisted with all its might. Ted frantically fumbled with the key. He could hear a muffled, high-pitched pulsing screech emanating from inside the room. The key entered the lock, and Ted forced it counterclockwise, releasing the deadbolt with a click. The barricade yawned ajar with the turn of the knob. The electronic squeal of his touch-tone telephone's ringer called out again. Ted shrugged the strap of his backpack from his right shoulder, letting the bag and its contents fall to the floor. He reached the phone with a swift, powerful stride. Picking up the receiver, he barked a quick "Hello?" into the speaker.

"Ted? It's Kate."

"Hi!" He slid into the nearest seat, his black vinyl beanbag chair. The material let out a groan under his weight. "What's up?"

"I called to thank you," she explained. "They're beautiful!"

Ted closed his eyes, thinking of the sight of a dozen baby red roses, sitting in a vase on a coffee table or counter in Kate's family home.

"I'm looking at them now. I can't believe you did this!"

"So you like them?"

"Like 'em? I love them! My birthday pretty much sucked all day yesterday. Then I came home to these. They made my day. Thank you."

"No problem. I'm glad I made yesterday decent. What else did you do?"

"Well, my parents took me to The Olive Garden for dinner. It was cool; Mom came home early from the office and everything. And I got some money. Belinda's gonna help me spend it tomorrow."

"That's great. I think I'm going to a party in Dressler tomorrow night."

"Cool. Hey, which one's that?"

"It's the beer can on the right." Ted flipped a pink slip of paper around with his left hand. He read it, then dropped it back onto the desk's surface. A faint knock came from the vicinity of the doorjamb; Ted turned to spot Sam's portly build in the doorway. Ted quickly mumbled, "I gotta go."

"Do what?"

"Sorry. I need to go. Hey, happy birthday."

"Thanks. Talk to you later."

"Okay. Bye." Ted placed the receiver back on the hook and turned, facing his companion. "Sam, that was her."

"Yeah?" Sam scratched his chin.

"She loved 'em." Ted's teeth sparkled from his mouth in a wide grin.

"See? Told ya buddy." Sam turned to leave, then stopped. "You eaten yet?"

"No. Alleyway Grille okay?"

"Sounds good."

"Alrighty then." Ted hopped up from his seated position quickly. He generated a gust of wind with his movement. As he left, the gust picked up the pink slip of paper, which floated to the tiled floor. The note landed print side up. The sheet of paper read:

Chet's Flowers

One Dozen Baby Reds

Card To Read:

Kate, hope your birthday is as special and as meaningful as you are to me. Love, Ted.

10

April 30, 1993
But that's when you knew me.

Kate trotted down a flight of stairs, her short legs churning like pistons, her golden hair bouncing with life with each tread of her feet. She flashed a quick glance at a wall clock as she reached flat ground. 12:52! She needed badly to reach the bus before it left, especially on this day.

I can't miss my meeting. Get out of my way.

She stiffarmed the door, which was closing gently as she reached its oaken face. She scrambled past a tall, full-bearded gentleman in a camouflaged jacket and down a long wheelchair accessible ramp. Kate cut around the corner with a stutter and head fake that Barry Sanders would struggle to match. If she had theme music, it would undoubtedly be Tchaichovsky's *1812 Overture*, her darting in and out of crowds coinciding with the crashes of the cymbals. She glided across the concrete in a steep breakneck pace, with a strong gait.

Making good time.

Patterson Hall loomed on her left, overlooking her steady progress. She slowed briefly, clutching her backpack strap with her left hand. She shrugged her shoulder, repositioning the cumbersome knapsack in a more comfortable spot. Quickening her pace again, Kate felt the bag bounce off her body with each stride, clashing on her shoulderblade. Stride, bang, step, smack. She looked ahead, trying to anticipate her next hole, when she spotted a familiar build, a familiar walk, coming toward her.

The man she spotted strode fast, but not labored. His gangly, ridiculously long legs propelled him across great chunks of earth with relative ease. Pale blue jeans hung from his thin waist, in a straight taper toward his feet. A black pullover covered his torso. The zipper of the garment remained open; Kate spotted purple pinstripes on a white jersey shirt beneath the black top. His hands hid inside a front pouch on the black windbreaker's stomach. Dusty brown hair, parted on his right, her left, lifted and bobbed with each stride. His eyes stared into the earth at his feet.

She drew closer to the homely young man. "Ted!" she called, which served to raise his eyes from his intense study of the youthful blades of grass. She waved her right hand in the air, keeping a firm grip on the padded strap of her backpack with her left hand. He flashed his right hand skyward in return, with a motion like a salute. The two friends stopped mere feet apart.

"Kate. Hey." Ted flashed a smile.

"Hey Ted. How've you been?"

"Fine." He looked beyond her. "What've you been up to?"

"Not much. Just school. I'm done for today though." She glanced anxiously toward the Pence Union Building. Her left foot tapped on the sidewalk. "You got the time?"

"Sure." Ted pulled both hands from his pouch. He launched his right arm out until it fully extended, a snap of his elbow exposing his watch from beneath the cuff of the windbreaker. He cocked his right elbow and presented his wrist to Kate.

She stared at Goofy's happy face, dumbfounded. "Ted," she asked, "uh...how come your watch says it's 11:05?"

"Wha?" he queried, pulling his arm toward his line of sight. "No, silly," he laughed, "this watch runs the other way. It says five 'til one."

"Oh. I guess I have a few minutes then." Her mouth curled in a nervous frown.

Ted's head tilted slightly to the left. "You in a hurry?"

"Yeah, yeah I am." Kate kicked her left foot at a clod of dirt. "You remember how I didn't know what I wanted to do? Well, I've found something I like."

"Really? That's great! What?"

"I'm really liking Intro to Sociology and Psych 101. It's so fascinating, studying the human mind. I love reading about our behavior, how come we decide to do the things we do, what makes us tick inside. And I'm gettin' great grades in both classes. I just seem to be good at it. This is something I think I could see myself doing for my career. So I've decided. I'm going to get my degree in psychology…"

"That's great!"

"At Whitworth." The sun ducked behind a darkening cloud. Ted swallowed hard, holding down the urge to scream, to vomit, to run away. His nostrils snorted hot air.

"Besides," Kate continued, "I've never fit in here anyway. It's too long to commute, none of my friends are here. I'll live at school, only have to go five minutes to go home. I won't be so burnt. Belinda's gonna be my roommate. That's where I'm headed today, to meet with an adviser, set everything up."

Ted's stomach knotted, as if he'd been kicked squarely in the testicles.

"This is best for me. I haven't been myself since high school. In fact, these past two years have been the worst two years of my life." These words felt like a left hook to the body. "It's been nothing but sadness." A right to the jaw. "I haven't been myself. In fact, I've hate myself here." An uppercut, and the challenger is down! "But now, I can get back on track. It's really for the best."

Ted gulped air, ran his sweaty hands through his hair. "It sounds like…you…know what you want. I'm glad for you." The lie burned his tongue like hydrochloric acid.

"I do. You know, I'll probably have to come back though."

"You will?" The sun reemerged from behind a gray cloud.

"Yeah probably. I'll probably want to get my Master's Degree in education. Eastern's the best school in the region for that type of degree. If I decide to go that route, it'll likely be here. Oh crud! What time is it?"

Ted glanced at his watch. "Goofy says it's one o'clock."

"Thank you Goofy." Kate stepped past Ted, then turned in midstride. "See you later," she said, waving a happy hand. Ted threw a halfhearted limb in her general direction, letting the lifeless slab of flesh fall by his side. Menacing gray clouds collided overhead, joining their forces to choke out the light of the sun. Ted watched Kate steadily grow smaller and out of focus, until she eventually blended into the crowd. He turned and continued his walk toward downtown Cheney.

My friends aren't here.

Ted followed the sidewalk, mainly with his eyes. A short Asian male passed him on the right, in the grass. The Asian's tiny legs worked a yeoman's workload compared to Ted's lazy American strides. Ted thought about an old skit he once saw—was it "Saturday Night Live"?—about a book called *Kicked in the Butt By Love*.

Maybe I could still order that book.

I've hated myself here.

Ted raised his eyes, looked left. He passed by Hargreaves Hall, a three-story brick building. A woman rolled down a ramp in her wheelchair, pushing narrow tires with her fingertips. She applied a hand brake as she reached the end of the ramp, a squeal of rubber and metal as she turned right. Ted continued walking, picking up the pace a little as he passed by the antique building.

As he continued wandering, dazed, toward town, he looked around quickly at objects. Every time he focused on one thing, two words seemed to echo from inside his head.

At Whitworth.

He stared at a charcoal colored iron statue, one that supposedly represented a full-grown woman but only stood maybe three feet tall. A small fence surrounded the statue, some sort of monument to some important figure long since dead.

At Whitworth.

Senior Hall rested on its foundation, left of the sweeping sidewalk that cut through campus. A two-story house, the hall perplexed Ted every time he happened by it. Were there classes in there? Did the dean live there? Or did it just sit empty? Whatever the hall was used for, it needed a new coat of paint nonetheless.

At Whitworth.

Ted watched a burgundy station wagon pass in front of him, then trotted across the street, stifflegged. He hopped the curb, then returned to his previous pace. Cresting a hill, Ted peered down at Cheney's retail district. He fixed his eyes on a series of grain silos, connected together to form one large receptacle. Painted pale mint green, the silos clashed harshly with orange-brown hills behind the collective on the horizon. The grain elevator probably existed before the current town and would likely stay, especially longer than Ted wanted to.

At Whitworth.

Faint sprinkles impacted the blacktop, impacted rooftops, trees, grass, Ted. He pulled a thin black hood over his scalp. Ted followed the crown of the road, choosing to walk the center of the vacant street instead of the sidewalk. Droplets of water started to fall more frequently. Ted walked on, his mind in other places.

At Whitworth.

11

June 1, 1993
Oh what a night, early June back in '93, it was her and baby it was me, yes indeed oh what a night.

Ted sighed heavily, reading from a European History textbook. He held a Bic pen in his teeth and a highlighter in his fist. He sat Indian style on his bed, the book in his lap, his shoulders hunched over, and his lower back against the bricks. Ted squinted at a passage in low light. Only the wall lamp expelled light; most of the room remained cold, dark, quiet. Tossing the book aside, Ted uncrossed his legs and rose to his feet.

"I gotta get outta here," he mumbled to the wall, tugging a red sweatshirt off his chest and over his head. The sweatshirt flew across the room, landing in a broken heap on the floor near the dresser. Ted slipped his head through the unzipped neck of his black pullover windbreaker. Adjusting the zipper to about halfway, he looked into the vanity mirror above the dresser. Any hairs out of place were quickly fixed after Ted licked his fingertips and rolled the digits through his locks. Turning toward the door, he snatched the key ring in his left fist and strode toward the door.

Pulling the door shut behind him, Ted tested the knob to make sure it held. Satisfied, he turned left, heading toward the elevator lobby.

Burnt orange carpet led the way like a crusty orange brick road. Ted followed the path intently with his eyes, crossing five seams and three worn spots until his instincts told him to turn right. Licking his dry lips, Ted stopped at a silver water fountain. He snatched the faucet, turning it away from his body. A prismatic rainbow of water arced into the air, dropping over a basin and emptying directly into a circular drainage grate. Ted inched forward, then lowered his labia until they touched fluoridated refreshment. Icy cold, the water splashed into Ted's mouth, stored there momentarily until he swallowed. The steady crystalline stream ceased as Ted released his grip on the faucet. The last remnants of the flow swirled down the drain as Ted swallowed one final load of cold, clear water. His partially numbed tongue flashed out, lapping clean his upper lip like a windshield wiper. Looking to his right, he noticed Bianca standing in an adjoining corridor.

"Ted. There you are. I was coming to get you," she announced. She approached, her chunky waddle powering her forward. Sighing, Ted waited for her to engage him. Bianca strode to him, then positioned herself between Ted and the elevator lobby he so desperately wished to enter. However inadvertent her intent, Bianca had, in effect, forced Ted to talk to her.

"So," she continued, "I have that ramen all ready for you. Come get it from me."

"Now?" Ted asked, a hint of surprise masking his supreme desire to have nothing to do with her at the moment. He took a step in reverse, then felt a flat, polished surface against his back. Looking at his toes, he noticed a thin plastic strip extending from under his left foot. His right foot stood on a tiled floor, similar in color to the tiles in his dorm room but cut into smaller squares. Bianca had backed him into the door of the laundry room with her choice to close the proximity between them. Ted looked up, telling her, "I'll come by in a little while. I was just on my way out," as he raised his face to hers.

"No. It can't wait until later." Bianca stepped forward and shifted slightly to her right with a subtle step. She now blocked both corridors with her girth, at least partially. "I might be gone later," she continued. "Come get it now."

"Oh, I see," Ted responded, his mouth curling into a scowl while his eyes darted back and forth, looking for a means of escape. A high-pitched giggle reverberated down the hallway to Ted's left, the hallway he had tread just seconds before, the hallway he wished he still occupied. "I should come right now, 'cause you say so. I should just drop whatever I might have planned for your convenience. Is that right?"

"Well. Yeah," Bianca replied, selfish pride resonating in her voice.

"Go to Hell, you bitch." Ted's fists balled tightly; his eyes narrowed into evil slits. He bullied his way through Bianca with a swift shoulder check, spinning her around on the ball of her right foot. Ted marched with a quick, determined pace, choosing the stairs over the elevator this time.

Eyes blazing fire, Ted stalked down the hallway toward the distant portal to his freedom. Traci, Sam, and Cassie scrambled into the hallway, midway between Ted and his goal. They giggled; Sam held a cup in his right hand. Cassie wielded a hair dryer, the white power cord dangling from her grip toward the carpet. She playfully pointed the blower at Sam's temple. Sam feigned like he planned to throw the contents of the full cup in Cassie's direction. He was oblivious to Ted's presence until Ted passed him in the hall. Traci escaped the threat of the water bath by ducking into the passageway to the left, a hallway halfway to Ted's goal. She laughed maniacally; the three of them cackled uncontrollably. Ted continued his power march to the far door.

"Ted?" chuckled Cassie, now a few short inches in front of and to the right of the doctor's eldest son. She pointed the hair dryer toward Ted's skull, giggling madly as she extended her arm. Ted flashed out his right hand, palming the device at the attached diffuser. Without breaking stride, Ted violently pushed the impediment from his path. Cassie winced in pain, dropping the hair dryer to the carpet. The diffuser popped from the nozzle, rolling across the hallway until it stopped against a set of double doors that concealed the trash bins. Ted remained focused forward, finally reaching his destination. The hallway fell silent as he opened the door.

"What's wrong with him?"

"I don't know."

"It's not like him."

All three of Ted's friends quickly discussed the moment, huddled together in the hallway. Ted turned toward the trio of voices as he began to pass into the stairwell. Six eyes stared back at him, large as satellite dishes. He blinked back in their general direction. The blaze in his eyes smoldered for a brief split second, then was quenched by the deluge of tears in his eyes.

At Whitworth.

After working his way through the labyrinth of hallways, staircases, and lobbies to the front vestibule of Morrison Hall, Ted climbed a short hill, crossing the street as he reached the crest. Two deep, muddy tire ruts led from the pavement into short grass, blocked from through traffic with a single chain, sagging between two thin posts, that bowed toward the earth. Ted hurdled the chain, then followed the tire tracks about ten feet, to their conclusion. A concrete structure stood before him; actually, only about three to four feet extended skyward above the earth. Ted didn't know what the structure housed, if anything, but he believed it somehow connected to the cylindrical tank nearby, all but seven feet of which was also buried below ground. The rectangular fortress before him brought back memories of bunkers on Fairchild Air Force Base, sights from his ancient past. The popular choice among the students, however, was that the rectangular building filtered water from the cylinder, then piped it to the campus from its high perch overlooking Cheney.

Ted swung his right leg onto the flat roof of the structure, then pulled himself up. Even in the rapidly advancing darkness of the last evening in May, he could still make out the red and black checkerboard pattern painted on the flat surface. Retreating from the faint light of the setting sun, Ted wandered to a far corner, which faced northeast. The general direction Kate lived in.

At Whitworth.

Ted took a seat at the corner, letting his left leg dangle to the north, his right leg to the east. He leaned back until his back lay flat on the concrete, and he stared into the dimly lit, yet rapidly illuminating, starry sky. He sobbed dryly a few times, then decided not to cry and stopped the tears. After a month's worth of the same night, Ted knew how to shut off his emotions when he wanted to. He stared at the stars for a long while as they grew stronger, him in the same prone position, his arms resting with interlocked fingers behind the crook of his neck.

A cavalcade of different ideas floated throughout his mind during the half hour he sat there. Images of Kate's face passed through, her golden locks shining in the sunlight. Thoughts of his grandfather came and went, the grandfather Ted looked like, the grandfather who Ted missed out on enjoying the company of before he died. Sometimes Ted believed he could see Granpa looking down at him from the sky; nothing but stars met Ted's gaze on this night as he stared blankly into space. Memories of different, insignificant events stumbled around inside his head, memories of chance meetings, of parties, of good times. Most of all, the horrors of that day, an entire month ago but only a blink away, defied his best efforts to evade them. All those words stung his ears; all their meaning tore open his chest. "She's gone, and I can't do a thing about it," he muttered to the twinkling pinholes in the night sky.

He sat up at that moment, forcing himself to one knee and to his feet. He stared out into the surroundings, past the red beacon blinking atop the outline of a bulbous water tower. His eyes passed over the fields beyond the houses. By day, the horizon looked like a patchwork quilt, squares of green connected with scraps of tan, a border of forest green surrounding the edges. At night, it was dark with darker and a border of darker still. He scanned the skyline, then stopped when he faced northeast. The general direction Kate lived in.

"At home."

Like a porchlight at a farmhouse, the distinction between the two lit up Ted's mind. Ted's shoulders straightened, his chin rose from its burrow in his chest. His slumped back lifted, and his eyes cleared from their glossy haze. And, for the first time in nearly one month, Ted smiled.

She's not gone. I can still have her, even if it's only for one night.

He turned, half running, half walking, toward the dormitory. With a quick hitch step, Ted bounded from the raised flat surface to the grassy knoll, then stutterstepped before jogging across the street. His chin held high, Ted reentered the building. His toes tickled the tile in a vibrant stride. Greeting the resident adviser on call, he passed the desk and glided to the elevators. Nothing could stop him now, not even, perhaps, Kate saying no.

Flipping his key ring like a gunfighter's pistol on his finger, he caught the right key and slid it effortlessly into the lock. The door gave way graciously. Ted strutted to the phone, dialing seven digits he knew by heart. The door remained ajar; Ted wanted the world to hear this. The connection rang three times, then a breathless "Hello?" crackled into the receiver.

"Hello. Is Kate there please?"

"This is. Who's this?"

"Hey Kate, it's Ted." His voice hurried the greeting from his mouth.

"Hey! Wassup?"

No time like the present. "Well, I called to see…if…we could go to dinner tomorrow night?"

"Um, Ted, I don't know…I have some work to do…but…" *come on please!* "Yeah. I guess so." Ted fumbled the phone but recovered before dropping the receiver.

"Okay great! I'll…um…meet you…uh…"

"How about at Northtown? Meet me…oh I know! There's a bench out in front of Kit's Cameras. You know where that is?"

"Oh, yeah," Ted lied, "So…how's six?"

"That's fine. I just need to be home by nine."

"Okay. Fair enough. See ya tomorrow." Ted hung up the telephone and worked to gain control of his racing heart. Once his heartbeat was contained, he pumped his fist in the air. He snatched a short, dark remote control, pointing it at his stereo. With the touch of a button, he started a compact disc and celebrated by wiggling happily to the beat.

* * *

"Hey Ted." Cassie filled half the doorway with her narrow hips. She tapped her lavender fingernails on her faded jeans shorts. After a second of waiting for a response, she continued, her thick, curly ponytail bobbing with her words. "Ted, are you hungry? I need someone to eat with."

"Sorry. I can't," Ted replied, tucking a blue dress shirt into his jeans.

"Are you mad at me?" Cassie put her left hand on her left hip, casting a defiant shadow.

"No," Ted replied, dumbfounded. "Why do you ask?"

"Well, first, you threw my hair dryer out of my hand yesterday. You just stormed off after it happened. Now you won't come get some dinner with me. It seems to me I did somethin' wrong." She stepped into the room, then rested her left thigh on Ted's unmade bed.

Ted brushed a wire comb through his hair. He talked to Cassie through the vanity mirror. "I'm sorry. I'm not mad at you. Bianca pissed me off yesterday, then you got in the way when I tried to leave. As for dinner, I'd love to…believe me…but…"

"But what?"

"I'm goin' to dinner with my friend Kate tonight." Cassie's mouth fell open. Ted turned to her, raising his arms to either side, stretching the dress shirt to wear more comfortably while tucked in. "Do I look all right?"

Cassie shook her head, returning to reality. "Oh, sure, except…" she paused while scratching her chin, "you need to iron that."

"I don't have an iron."

"But I do. Come on." Cassie snatched Ted's left arm, pulling him from his room and down the hallway to the laundry room. Once there, she instructed him to remove his blue Eddie Bauer dress shirt while she filled the iron with water and plugged in the unit.

Ted sat on top of the dryer, which vibrated and squeaked with activity. He tugged nervously at the sleeve of the plain white T-shirt that draped his thin trunk. Cassie worked on the dress shirt, running the iron over its surface. Teresa, the resident adviser for the third floor, arrived with an orange basket under one arm.

"Wassup guys?" she greeted, a flurry of fast hands. Teresa's dark, kinky hair was pulled behind a white headband. She emptied the washer, removing T-shirts from the cylinder. Faint dots of moisture landed on her gray Nike sports bra and glistened off satin Umbro shorts, the brightest red that could be found. She took her pile of shirts and deposited them next to Ted on the dryer, then produced two quarters and placed them into a sliding tray on the washer. She pushed the tray in, creating life in the quiet beast. After a few seconds, Teresa opened the lid, stopping the steady filling of the washer. Grainy soap cascaded into the unseen chasm, then the lid dropped again, giving life once more. Teresa pushed her damp shirts into the orange basket, to wait their turn to ride in the warm air of the dryer.

Cassie waited for Teresa to finish her task, then spoke up. "Ted's got a date!" she announced, bouncing as she made her proclamation. "I'm ironing for him now!"

Teresa squealed "Omigosh! Ted?" while reaching out to give him a hug. Ted hopped from the dryer, accepting her friendly embrace. She released him, holding his shoulders from arm's length, grinning widely. "Who's the lucky lady?"

"It's not a date," Ted sheepishly replied. "She's just a friend. We're going to dinner and maybe some other stuff."

"Ooh, some other stuff." Teresa winked, then joined Cassie's laughter with her own. "Lessee, dinner and other stuff. Yep, it's a date."

"Yep," concurred Cassie, "date."

"Okay," Ted reluctantly agreed, "fine. It's a date."

"Well, best of luck. When is it?"

"I gotta meet her at six o'clock. I have about ten minutes before I havta go."

Teresa turned to go, but stopped as she reached the open laundry room door. "Hey, you smell terrific! What is that?"

Ted's cheeks turned pink, a shy smile crossing his face. "It's Right Guard. I've got about four cans of the stuff on today."

"Huh. Well, I hope you have a good time tonight."

"Me too. I'll tell you all about it when I get back."

Cassie swept the shirt one last time, then shimmied the garment off the ironing board. She carefully handed the shirt to Ted, like a squire presenting a knight with his sword. Ted slipped his arms into the sleeves, then buttoned down the shirt and tucked blue tails into his jeans.

Ted spun his key ring on his finger, leaving the laundry room with Cassie close behind. Once in the hallway, Ted turned to Cassie. She opened her arms, wrapping them around him. No words were exchanged; they said everything that needed to be said with the hug. As they released the embrace, Ted noticed Sam approaching from down the corridor. With a quick "Wassup?" he backed away from Cassie.

"Wassup with me? What's with you, all dressed up?" Sam rubbed his chin, studying Ted's executive shoes and casual blue button-down shirt.

"Remember my friend Kate I told you about? We're having dinner tonight."

"You dog! Here then." Sam fished a leather billfold from the left front pocket of his dark cargo pants, then flipped it open. He licked his fingers, then reached deep into the wallet's compartments. After a quick search, his stubby digits produced an object, a red circle of translucent material in a clear square of plastic.

"Thanks, but no," Ted said, nodding his head and waving his hands in disagreement. "I don't need a jimmy hat tonight. That's not what tonight's gonna be about."

Sam stroked the condom between his thumb and index finger. He moved the prophylactic into his open palm while he struggled to open his wallet with his left hand. With a sudden flash, Cassie snatched the protective latex from his hand, commenting with a "Yoink!"

"Just like a slut," Sam chuckled, replacing his wallet in his pocket. "No matter how many times a man leaves ya, you always seem to land on your back." Cassie slapped his chest playfully, unoffended by the joke, a wry smile decorating her narrow face. Regaining his faculties, Sam patted Ted's left shoulder. "Good luck buddy," he encouraged, a sparkle of pride in his pupils. Ted thanked Sam and Cassie, then entered the elevator lobby and boarded a waiting carriage.

* * *

Ted pushed a cassette into the tape deck, then used his right hand to give the black volume knob a clockwise nudge. Upbeat music filled the cabin. Ted tapped his fingers on the steering column, singing along with the selection. He had spent half the afternoon preparing this particular mix tape, carefully selecting tunes that made him happy while at the same time helping him redirect his nervous energy into something positive. However, as the 1990 Ford Thunderbird streaked like a white chariot on eastbound Interstate 90, the steady drumming of his fingers slowed. As the tall grasses in his peripheral vision changed over to lush green pines and firs, his singing ceased.

Every second with her is one second closer to the last one.

The song concluded, then there was silence. Ted flashed a glimpse in the rearview mirror, noticing his eyes. Heavy, foggy, tired orbs looked back at him. He pressed and held a lever on his left armrest, which lowered the driver's side window, allowing the tension to escape the automobile. A new song filled the car, a healthy layering of samples and drum machines. Two lines into the lyrics, Ted flashed another look in the mirror. His corneas shone brightly, his irises a brilliant teal blue. His eyes looked young, light, vibrant. Rolling up the window, Ted began to follow loudly with the lyrics, repeating each word with great vigor and energy.

"It's not the end," he whispered to Granpa, "but the beginning."

Pines and firs gave way to hotels, then tall signs and even taller buildings. The Thunderbird effortlessly transversed the freeway exit, swinging a left turn onto Division. Following a northerly path, the white sports coupe, clad in a black hood bra, began to climb a steady incline lined by business after business on either side.

The hill flattened as an intersection approached. Ted directed the T-bird through a green light, then pressed a lever on the steering column, which created a low, intermittent clicking and a flashing green arrow on the dashboard pointing to the right. Spinning the wheel clockwise, Ted entered a large parking lot. Other automobiles lay scattered about, in partitions marked with white paint over blacktop. Ted applied steady pressure to the brake pedal, then allowed the car to roll slowly as he cranked the steering wheel to the right. More pressure to the brakes, and the Thunderbird halted in a parking stall, nose to nose with a green Ford Taurus. Ted pressed a thumbsized button, holding the contraption in while he moved a thick handle from "D" to "P"; all the while, he held constant pressure on the brake pedal with his right foot. The lever locked in place, effectively keeping the car from moving any farther. Releasing the pressure on the pedal, Ted twisted and removed the key from its entrapment in the ignition switch. He flashed a quick peek at himself in the rearview mirror. From this glance, he shifted his attention to the entrance to the building that stood sentry behind him. Ted reached for a plastic handle molded in smoke gray, then pulled the handle, allowing the car door to swing open. Planting both feet upon the blacktop, Ted lifted his body from the cabin of the automobile.

Let's do this.

Ted took slow, deliberate steps as he approached the entrance to Northtown Mall. Panels of glass stood three stories high, allowing natural light into each level of the complex. Ted looked briefly toward the roof, then trained his eyes on the doors. Two sets of glass doors, each set consisting of two doors side by side, awaited him as he crossed onto a cement sidewalk. He reached out with his right hand and grasped a C-shaped handle on one of the doors. He opened the door with a gentle push, and he quickly passed through the portal into a glass vestibule. Holding the door, Ted waited for a lady to push a stroller out to the concrete, then allowed the glass to shut on its own. Surrounded by glass and steel, Ted stepped across bone tan carpeting and reached for the interior set of double doors. Once more he pushed through with little effort, slowing in response to the crisper air inside the building, obviously the work of the air conditioning. He stopped as he cleared the door's path. A gasp of air tickled his neck as the door torqued on a spring mechanism before closing at a controlled speed.

Ted scanned the expansive mall before him, looking for his pre-arranged rendezvous point with Kate. His eyes followed the wall to his left, passing a couple storefronts until he noticed a small, cramped establishment. He took one step toward the narrow shop. The entrance was flanked by two glass display windows, then a dark charcoal border of large tiles that resembled blocks. Above the entrance, an illuminated sign read "Kit's Cameras" in yellow. Ted's eyes darted right. They stopped in the middle of the floor, in the foreground of the long corridor before him.

An ornate wooden bench faced away from the camera shop, toward a delicatessen. Couples and families sat at a series of tables, both inside and in front of the restaurant. Ted's focus returned to the bench, its curved back beckoning him to recline underneath the shade of a thin tree planted in an immense pot. The thin tree sat to the immediate left of the bench, beyond the oblong seat from Ted's point of reference. Ted swallowed his nervous pinings, stepping toward the wooden bench. He turned and lowered himself onto the crossbeams of thin, molded wood. Lifting his right foot, Ted rested the foot on his left knee, scratching his ankle through a white athletic sock. Happy with the results of his anxious itching, Ted placed his left elbow on the elegantly carved wooden armrest that bookended the bench. Leaving his right foot on his left knee, he gazed at his loafers for a moment, then turned his head to the left, transfixing his gaze on an approaching figure.

Kate stopped a few feet in front of him. Saying her hello, she sat next to him, on his right. Ted followed her with his eyes. Her goldenrod locks swept behind her ears, held at the center of her scalp by an amber berette. The hair cascaded down her neck to her shoulders. A white Arrow shirt covered her torso, with a green sleeveless sweater pulled over it. The sweater plunged in a V in the neck; Kate left the top two buttons undone on the white shirt beneath the sweater. A necklace rounded her neck, with a charm, a half-circle with a jagged left side, falling below her windpipe. Black dress slacks hugged her hips, then hung flat around her legs to her feet. She wore saddle shoes, the kind with black toes and heels and white panels of patent leather in the middle. As she sat, she carefully placed a black handbag between her and Ted, the strap slipping between two thin slats.

"You look very nice today," Ted commented, brushing his sweaty palms through his hair, refusing to remove his gaze from her brilliant blue eyes. Uncrossing his legs, he lifted to a standing position, a move Kate copied. She slung her purse over her left shoulder, then grasped Ted's right arm and gently squeezed.

"Ted," she explained, "I hope this doesn't bother you, or ruin any plans you had, but I need to get home by about nine o'clock. I still have some work to finish."

"Sure," Ted replied, no visible hints of disappointment apparent. "I thought we'd get some dinner, then go from there. Nothing set in stone, I thought we'd play it by ear."

"Phew. I thought you'd be upset." Kate nodded her appreciation as Ted held open the inner of the two sets of doors they needed to pass through to reach the parking lot.

"Upset? Nah'l." Ted took quick steps, then opened the second door. "I'm just happy I get to see you today."

They crossed the parking lot, arriving at the white Thunderbird. Ted effortlessly unlocked and opened the passenger door, swiftly trotting around the front of the car seconds later and sliding the key into the lock on the driver's side. Within seconds he was behind the wheel, Kate mere inches to his right. He inserted the key into the ignition, then turned the key clockwise ninety degrees.

The engine purred to life, drowned out by the earshattering volume of the stereo system. "Sorry! My bad!" Ted shouted, clumsily turning the volume control knob left, reducing the noise to a more acceptable level. He ejected the mix tape, tossing it underneath his seat on the floorboard. Ted put the car into reverse and backed out of the spot, then shifted into drive and left the parking lot, turning right onto Wellesley Avenue and right again onto Division.

Kate pulled down the sun shade on the passenger side of the car and lifted a rectangular hatch to expose a vanity mirror. "So," she remarked, inspecting her light foundation and subtle lipstick, "what did you have in mind for dinner?"

"Well, I've had sort of a craving for seafood all week. I know I don't have a lot of cash, and you probably don't wanna spend anything, so I thought that place up by your house would work." Ted checked the rearview mirror. "Unless you have a better idea."

"Um…no…I, that sounds fine. It's your show." Kate eased deeper into the leather upholstery. She looked at her thin companion for a second, then shifted to watching the stores pass by.

After a few minutes, the Ford crested a hill and descended toward a fork in the highway. Ted chose the left fork, but almost immediately made a right turn, at the first opportunity he encountered. The car climbed a fast incline, followed quickly with a tight loop around a mahogany building. Ted settled the car into a space overlooking the highway that led to the fork they had just passed through a moment before. Ted began to reach for the keys when Kate stopped his progress.

"Look over there," she commented, shaking her right index finger in the general direction of a one-story silver-gray building across the four-lane road in front of them. "What about that place?"

Ted waited for a tractor trailer to pass, then noticed a red neon sign near the right end of the structure. It flashed on, reading "Chef Wok", then flashed off again. Ted rubbed his chin briefly. He slid his right hand to the lever and pushed it into the reverse position. "That's a good idea," he agreed, maneuvering the car toward the exit. Intently watching traffic, he gauged an opening and darted across four lanes with the gentle pressure of his foot, requesting turbocharged power. The T-bird bounced into Chef Wok's parking lot, coming to rest, with Ted's urging, in front of the business.

A tiny bell chimed weakly as the two friends entered the establishment. Kate and Ted quickly perused the restaurant. They glanced briefly at tables in a seating area which took up the right two-thirds of the business. A wall, standing about four feet high and painted eggshell white, separated the dining area from the main counter. A Formica counter extended about 18 inches from the left side of the white wall, a silver counter covered with bins and dispensers that held straws, napkins, chopsticks, utensils, and a variety of sauces and condiments. Carpeting ended at the wall, and exposed tile made up the floor where the greatest amount of foot traffic tread. Ted and Kate shuffled across the tiles, in a diagonal step toward the left, until they stood in front of a dull cash register, a silver-gray machine resting on a dark countertop.

"Welcome to Chef Wok," a carrot-haired woman greeted, squinting through thick glasses at the duo. Her strong Southern accent bellowed through the empty Oriental restaurant. She wiped her hands on a cardinal apron tied around her waist. "How may I hawlp y'all?"

Kate ordered first, selecting teriyaki chicken and rice. Ted pulled crisp bills from his pocket, then reached out his fist of cash while Flo read the total aloud.

"Ted, I can't let you pay." Kate frowned, sounding disappointed that he'd made the gesture.

Ted shook his head. "Just let me do it. Please."

"Okay," Kate agreed, "but I will get you back someday." She dropped her wallet back into her purse.

Ted turned his attention to the counter. "An' I'll have chicken stir fry."

"Excellent choice. Y'all'll get your food in a quick minute." The lady turned her back to the couple, drawling "Clarence!" to an empty window. After a few seconds, a younger Caucasian gentleman in a red bib apron appeared, spatula in latex-gloved hand. Flo relayed the order, and Clarence disappeared into the mysterious catacombs behind the wall.

Ted sat at a rectangular table, chuckling in a hushed tone to himself. "What's so funny?" Kate asked, her head and upper torso visible from behind the short wall of helpful items.

"Oh, nothing," Ted giggled, "I'm just waiting for her to say 'Kiss mah grits!'" He trailed off as he spoke, consciously trying not to be heard.

"Do what?" Kate asked , rounding the corner, packets of soy sauce and a bundle of chopsticks in her small hands.

"Oh, you know," Ted replied. "Flo from Mel's Diner. You didn't notice her name tag?"

"I did, but I don't think…oh! I get it now." Kate smiled, then started to laugh, a hollow snort that she tried to stifle by covering her mouth and nose with her hands. She made a high pitched squeal, which caused Flo to stare in her direction. Kate covered her rapidly flushing face in her hands, convulsing in a silent gleeful laugh. Ted smirked while watching the scene, then looked at Flo and threw up both hands with a shrug. Flo turned and disappeared into the back.

Kate regained her composure. "So what's up with you Ted?" she asked, struggling to control her breathing. "What're you doin' this summer?"

"Workwise, probably not much. I'll probably end up doing odd jobs around the house. Geoff and I're goin' to St. Louis at the end of the month for a few days."

"Really? What for?" Kate played with her packets of soy sauce, building a small pyramid with the stack.

"We're going to some baseball games mainly. It's Geoff's favorite team. We're goin' as a graduation gift to him." Ted glanced at the empty front counter.

Kate thought for a second. "Now…who's Geoff again?"

"He's my cousin. You met him last year. Remember? He was over the week after Spring Break…"

"Oh yeah! I sent him in the hall that one night."

"Yep. That guy." They both fell silent. Kate fondled her soy sauce packets while Ted scratched the corner of the table with his left thumb. They both kept their eyes focused on the hardwood surface of the table, studying their surreal reflections in the thick, glossy varnish finish. Ted's legs began to shake beneath the table.

The uneasy silence that filled the empty restaurant mercifully ended, pierced by the shrill call of a bell, the kind found in hotel lobbies at the front desk, the round dome with a small metal rod imbedded in the top. Clarence appeared in the open cutout for a second, dropping two steaming plates before vanishing. Flo emerged from the right, picked up the plates, and carried the meals to her customers.

"Here ya go sweeties," she announced, carefully placing the dishes on the table in front of the two patrons. Ted watched her leave, fighting the urge to smack her on her ample ass. He got up and wandered over to the Formica counter. His hands passed over the bins and baskets. He returned with two handfuls of goodies: a set of chopsticks, a fork, soy sauce packets, pepper, and hot mustard.

Kate lifted a chunk of meat to her mouth, pressed between two thin chopsticks by her thumb and forefinger. Ted stabbed at a slice of green pepper with his fork.

Kate swallowed the animal flesh. "Why don't you use your chopsticks?"

Ted glanced at the paper bundle to the right of his plate. "Well…I'm…I hadn't thought about it." He picked up the bundle, unsheathing a slender shaft of balsa wood from the paper. He cracked the column in two, then used his left hand to position the two sticks properly in his grip. The sticks clapped together twice, directed by his fingers. With a quick stabbing motion, he clasped a piece of chicken. Ted raised the flesh toward his mouth. Suddenly, the chopstick guided by his index finger slipped. The shred of chicken bounced off the table. It skipped off Kate's arm before impacting on the dark blue carpet, where it remained dormant. Ted picked up his fork, deadpanning, "That's probably why I use a fork."

Kate flashed a glance at the rapidly cooling chunk of cooked meat that rested against the instep of her left shoe. "You want that back?" she asked.

"Nah, thanks. You can have it." Ted impaled a slice of chicken with his fork.

* * *

"So…what now?" Kate pushed open the restaurant's thick oaken door, nudging it momentarily to make sure Ted caught it. He let the heavy wooden panel impact his shoulder, then pushed it open with his left hand. Kate turned to him, backpedaling, asking, "What's the plan?"

"Oh, um…I hadn't thought that far ahead. Actually though…" Ted opened the passenger door with a tug of the handle, "get in."

Kate slid into the plush leather chair. Ted pressed the door shut, then trotted around the front of the car. Kate reached across the cabin, unlatching the driver-side door. Ted flopped into the seat, starting the engine with the turn of the key. A simultaneous click of seatbelts, and the couple was on its way.

"So, what have you got in mind?" Kate asked, brow furrowed.

"It's kinda a surprise. B-but you'll like it I hope. It's one a' my favorite spots." Ted pulled two quick lefts, propelling the Thunderbird through the Y intersection and into a southbound glide on Division.

Ted turned up the stereo slightly; other than the music, the Ford's interior remained silent. Kate's back remained straight, barely making contact with the leather. She looked at her fingernail polish periodically, once in a while shifting her eyes to catch a quick glimpse of Ted. Most of the ride, she drummed her fingers lightly on her legs.

Meanwhile, Ted guided the automobile, his hands properly in position at ten and two. He looked out the windshield, occasionally averting his gaze to the rearview mirror. Looking right, he caught Kate's attention. She smiled nervously; he grinned back with confidence. A car dealership approached on the right side of Division. Ted flipped a lever on the steering column, producing a low, rhythmic clicking noise and a flashing green arrow, pointing right.

The Thunderbird turned right onto Wellesley, heading into a slowly sinking sun. Still staring forward, Ted opened his mouth. "So, tell me again about what you're doing next year."

"Do what?"

"You know, about going to school." At Whitworth.

"Oh." Kate stopped her constant fingernail drumming. "Well, I'm goin' to major in psychology. Whitworth's the best place in town with the degree I want, an' I can live closer to home. Then when I graduate, I'll probably go back to Eastern for a teaching Master's."

Ted applied the brakes, stopping the car at a red light. Watching the stoplight closely, he continued the conversation: "Sounds good. At least you know what you're doing."

"And you? Ted, what are you gonna do?"

"Well…" he paused, switching his right foot from the brake to the gas pedal in response to the light glowing bright green. The Thunderbird jolted to life, creating enough push to momentarily force the two passengers into the padding of the seats. The car regained weight balance, and the two passengers adjusted themselves back into their comfortable positions, except that Kate slouched deeper into her chair.

"I thought that…" Ted continued, "well, maybe I'd…well, I think I like the idea of teaching. You know, helping out young kids, something of importance. I think I might like doin' that."

"That seems like a good idea." Kate's left hand patted Ted's right leg lightly, just above his knee. Ted flashed a quick glance at his friend, then returned to concentrating on the beige Chevy in front of him. A school passed on the left, followed by an expansive field. A large tower, painted green and gold, stood in the field. It too soon grew distant behind the duo in the white Thunderbird. They passed a strip mall almost immediately thereafter. Once they were by the shopping center, the buildings began to grow smaller and fewer in number, the trees denser and larger.

Kate tried to find a decent song on the stereo while Ted continued to drive the Ford toward the descending sun. She settled on a country music station, which played a slow lament about a lost love or lost dog, perhaps both. Ted rolled his eyes at the electronic readout, but let the potential problem drop. *It's her night too,* he thought, *and I better let her have it.* A rather large structure loomed on the horizon, just right of the road the pair traveled.

The immense structure blocked out the steadily fading orb of the sun, creating an artificial twilight. The manmade obstacle, an oval bowl, stood vigil over a hospital, casting a nurturing shadow over the trauma center. Light standards extended from this mysterious building, looking like scarecrows against the rapidly fading sunlight. The Thunderbird rolled to a halt at a stoplight, then passed through the intersection as the traffic signal once again turned green.

Kate pointed to the structure. "Is that where we're headed? The stadium?"

Ted peered at the stadium. As he passed the complex, he said, "No, but now I know we're close." The car was bathed in a pale glow once more.

Kate huffed and folded her arms emphatically across her chest. "Then *where* are we going?"

"Patience my dear," Ted replied, a laugh in his voice. The car began a slow descent into a lush valley. The horizon was a green wall. Tombstones littered the ground to the right of the speeding vehicle, marble pillars and stone markers that blurred by.

The road ended, forking directly left and right. Ted spun the steering wheel counterclockwise as he negotiated the intersection, moving the car to the left. Kate fixed her eyes to the west, out the passenger window. Her eyes broadened, soaking in her surroundings.

Even through the thicket of pines and firs that lined the drive, Kate spotted the magnificent churning life in a twisting canyon. Water the color of a shiny new quarter flowed to the north, opposite of the direction the Ford traveled. Pockets of sunlight illuminated the flow with a brilliant nickel sparkle. White foam formed where the rushing water met with outcroppings and boulders, rocks polished smooth by decades upon centuries of uninterrupted onslaught by the raging river. A dense growth of timber remained untouched on the far bank, extending as far as Kate's eyes could determine into the background. The Thunderbird weaved its way around a series of curves and corners, finally coming upon a vacant lot of dirt overlooking the riverbed.

The two friends climbed out of the car. Ted began to lock the doors while Kate started toward the riverbank. Removing the key from the passengerside door lock, Ted caught sight of Kate, nearing a narrow suspension bridge constructed of wood and lashed together with thick wire cables.

"Kate! Not that way!" Ted projected his baritone voice, trying to carry it over the relentless, dull roar of the endless water. She turned and yelled "Why not?" then took a couple steps toward Ted and the Thunderbird. He motioned for her to join him with the curl of his right index finger. Making sure she was following, Ted started toward a giant boulder that rested about 40 yards away.

Walking side by side, Kate and Ted wandered past the large, oblong rock. Ted explained to Kate that it had been left there by an ancient glacier sometime during the Ice Age. Kate listened intently to the lecture. She stooped over and picked up a piece of stone that had dislodged from the outcropping. The stone was a light, chalky gray; Kate's fingers were dusted with a grainy powder. She tossed the rock back onto a pile of pieces, listening to it impact in the other fractured portions of rock. Ted stopped in his tracks, looking at a worn spot of dirt between two young pine trees. "There it is," he commented over his shoulder.

"Do what?" Kate stared blankly at the youthful pair of trees, then at Ted. He pointed to a second boulder, partially obscured behind the trees and concealed by the sheer bulk of the first boulder. Brushing aside a pine limb, Ted beckoned for Kate to join him. She hesitated for a second, but reluctantly respected his wishes.

They followed a dirty trail of gravel up the hill, between the two immovable boulders. Reaching the second rock, Kate stopped, in surprise. A series of steps had been built into the rock, most likely carved or sandblasted. Ted extended his hand, which Kate accepted and grasped. He steadied her uncertain steps, keeping her safe by helping to guide her up the tractionless granite. They reached the top, which also had been carved or blasted into an observation deck, a bowl shaped depression to look over the canyon from.

The raging Spokane River passed beneath them, snaking unabated into the distance around bends in both directions. Pines and Douglas firs lined either hillside, silent guardians of the rampaging treasure below. From where they stood, not one hint of civilization, save for the wooden foot bridge, could be seen.

"Ted," Kate murmured, "this…is beautiful."

Ted smiled in response, basking in the total joy Kate expressed in her wide eyes. "I know. That's why I like to come here so much. My parents used to bring John and me a lot when we were kids. We'd always come and walk around down here. I never really knew why back then but now I'm glad we did. This is one of the few reasons I came back to this town." Ted pointed at a rock formation that sat in the middle of the flowing river. "You know what that is right?"

"A rock?"

Ted stepped back, his mouth dropping open. "No, it's the Bowl and Pitcher!"

Kate studied his amazement for a moment, thinking of an answer. "Really? I didn't know that was it."

"You've never been here before?"

"No?"

"And you've lived here how long?"

"All my life." Kate hunched her shoulders, stuffing her hands sheepishly into her pockets.

Ted grew silent for a moment, looking for the right thing to say. He reached out, grasping Kate's shoulder with his right hand. He looked into her deep blue pools of eyes, saying quietly, "Well, now you can say you have seen it." Holding out his hand, he remarked, "C'mon. Let's go."

Once more, Ted guided Kate over the smooth steps. Once on steadier earth, they both wandered down the gravelly, dusty path and between two deciduous limbs. As they approached the white chariot, Kate stopped. Ted halted a stride later.

"So, you really like this place huh?" Kate asked, squinting briefly at the river behind him.

"Yep. It's one of my fondest childhood memories. I can come here and instantly go back to the good times." Ted pushed his left hand into his left pocket, digging for the car keys.

Kate thought for a minute while Ted produced the key ring. He took a step toward the car, stopping when Kate spoke.

"I wanna take you to my spot!" she exasperated over the crashing of water. Ted turned, noticing the smile on her lips.

"Okay." Ted scooped his hand, underhand, through the air. A glistening object arced toward Kate. Instinctively, she protected herself, catching the flying projectile with both hands. Opening her fists, she glanced at the silver metal ring, ornamented with four keys. She looked up at Ted.

He pointed to the Thunderbird. "We'll take my mom's car."

With a skip step, Kate walked toward the only vehicle in the parking area, keys in hand.

* * *

"Is this it?" Ted grinned widely, his head cocked to one side to see through the windshield better.

"It is."

Ted's eyes widened as he gathered in the entire scene. The car faced a large building, a warehouse of a retail establishment. Even in the advancing twilight, a rainbow of vibrant colors blazed across the store's front. A great sign, illuminated internally, covered the upper half of the building. A large cartoon character, a giraffe, grinned gaily from his perch high above the parking lot. Full of glee, Ted exclaimed, "It's Toys R Us!"

"That's right," Kate said, pushing open the car door. "You took me to one of your childhood favorites. Now it's time to get back to one a' mine."

Kate and Ted entered the building, crossing through a portal after an automatic door slid open in their presence. They entered a dark, narrow hallway filled with shopping carts, a picture of Geoffrey the giraffe greeting them with a warm smile. The hallway remained dimly lit; in fact, the only source of light came from the end of the corridor.

"I feel like skipping," Ted chortled.

"Don't let me stop you."

"Nah, I'll behave. For now."

They reached the end of the corridor and were bathed immediately in bright fluorescent light. The layout of the franchise remained true to the chain. Ted and Kate stood in a small area partitioned off by display fixtures, an area that contained candy, school supplies, and toys that were priced on close-out. The wall in this area, off the couple's left shoulders, held inexpensive items like party favors and plastic army men. Aisles upon aisles of merchandise spread out in front of the duo, extending from the front of the store into the background. To their right, a bank of cash registers waited for customers, a sparse minority staffed by cashiers in blue vest aprons with mustard lettering. A cage lined the front wall, the farthest right the two close friends could see. Kate tapped Ted on the shoulder, breaking his incessant humming of the Toys R Us theme song. She pointed left, then led the way to the child's Garden of Eden.

They walked a couple of rows, past bikes and trains and video games in the biggest toy store there is. Both of them took note of the electronics and other toys that were far more advanced than anything they used to own or even fantasized about. "You see," Kate explained, "my mom and dad worked long hours and we hardly ever got to spend time together, even on the weekends. But one Saturday a month, they'd bring me here to see the new toys and I'd get to pick out one. At the time it was cool 'cause I got a new toy, but now I think it was cool because I got to see Mom and Dad." She picked up a plush doll, giving the bear a hug. "That's why this is my favorite place." The teddy bear returned to its shelf, to party with its bear friends.

"You know," Ted wondered, "I use to come here with my parents also. There's a chance we were here at the same time once."

Kate face lit up. "Gosh, wouldn't that be kooky?"

"I bet it happened. I bet I was looking at G.I.Joes one day and you came down the aisle trying to find Barbie or something." Ted and Kate fell silent, then an eerie lack of noise settled over the pair. They passed through an aisle, making no sound, contemplating the possibility of having met somewhere before.

Could it be possible? they both thought simultaneously.

"Look!" they exclaimed together, both pointing down the next aisle. On a shelf, about half a foot from the floor, a wooden skateboard rested with its urethane wheels in the air. The pair of friends looked at each other, hesitated for a second, and approached the board. Ted picked up the plank, then placed it wheels down on the tiled floor.

"You used to skate?" Kate asked, watching Ted balance awkwardly on the board.

"Kinda." He pushed with his left foot. Coasting about ten feet, he grabbed onto a round support beam, knocking a red courtesy telephone free of its mooring. Replacing the phone quickly, he commented, "These trucks need to be tightened." Turning, he asked, "Did you skate?"

"Sorta. I'd make up my own tricks in my driveway. I had this one trick I called the Special K where I'd put both hands on the ground and kick turn the skateboard. I usually fell on my butt though."

"Hey, I think my friend did the same kind of thing but called it the Tractor Taylor."

Ted turned the board around, kicking it softly with his toe, so it faced toward the front of the store. He pushed off the floor, gliding past Kate, spouting a "Watch this" as he coasted by.

Tensing on sinewy legs, Ted rose to his toes. He transferred his weight to his right leg, the leg to the rear of the skateboard's deck. Kicking with his dominant right leg, Ted raised the nose of the board, then lifted the tail. The skateboard escaped gravity by a couple inches, losing contact with the floor. Suddenly, the skateboard caught flight, hurtling like a rocket down the aisle. Ted also took to the air, his legs going parallel with the tiles. He landed on his bony buttocks, skipping off the floor from the impact. The skateboard glanced off the quarter panel of a battery operated pink plastic Jeep, then flipped and landed, belly up, in the aisle. The urethane wheels continued spinning. Ted lifted himself to a seated position. Giggling softly, he announced to the store, "Cleanup in Aisle Five!"

Kate planted herself on the shelf the skateboard originated from, her elfish frame doubled over in laughter. She tried to hide her rapidly flushing face in her tiny hands. Meanwhile, Ted giggled crazily from his seated position, hardly able to breathe. He turned to look behind himself and, through his own watering eyes, found Kate's hunched over body, convulsing in jubilation. A lady pushed a stroller past, between the two friends, shaking her head. Ted lifted his knees toward his chest, resting his elbows on his two knobby patellae.

Regaining her composure after great difficulty, Kate rose to her feet and strode to Ted. She sat down next to him, crossing her legs Indian style, and put her right arm across his broad shoulders. Looking at his profile, she said, "That was the funniest thing I think I have ever seen. Thank you."

"I'm glad you liked it," Ted replied, still facing toward the front of the retailer, eyeing a pimply-faced male blue vest and a portly female blue vest that stared at him.

"I did. I have. I've enjoyed the whole evening."

Ted turned his head left, making eye contact with Kate. "Me too," he replied.

The two of them both drew in a quiet breath, remaining silent in their seated positions. Ted heard nothing around him, not the hum of the lights, the faint squeak of plastic wheels on tile, the chatter of the blue vests, nothing. The only sound that filled his ears was the steadily increasing thuhpump, thuhpump of his own heart. He lost himself in Kate's cavernous blue eyes, hypnotized by their brilliant, sparkling glow.

Kate looked through Ted's teal blue eyes into his soul. She witnessed a deeply caring man, a great guy who could always be counted on. Her hand tensed on his shoulder. All the background noise dissipated beneath the sound of her own quickening heartbeat.

They each sat on the floor, silent, studying each other's eyes. Finally, after a couple minutes, each like a separate thousand lives, Kate blinked repeatedly. She glanced toward Ted's wrist, asking, "Ted? What time is it?" Her heartbeat slowed to a more comfortable, relaxed pace, and the low hum of fluorescent lighting and voices of the blue vests filled her ears.

Ted blinked back to reality. His heartbeat receded back to a slower pace; his ears filled with a myriad of noises, sounds of voices and activity around him. He snuck a peek at his watch, assuring Kate, "Goofy says it's a quarter 'til nine." He felt extra weight lift from across his shoulders.

"Ted, I gotta get going. I have an econ paper I still need to finish." Kate climbed to her feet, brushing the seat of her black pants with her open palms. Ted got up, lightly patting his jeans. Bending over, he collected the skateboard from its resting place near the Power Wheels and bigwheels. He stepped lively, skateboard under arm, to the low shelf he had originally retrieved it from and placed it carefully on its spot, among its fellow skateboards. Spinning on his right heel, Ted rejoined Kate, and the two best friends marched together toward the exit.

A menacing twilight sky greeted the couple once outside. During twilight in Spokane, especially in the summer months, the sky would invariably look like a torrential downpour was eminent. Even with not one cloud in the sky, sheets of rain seemed inevitable. A cold, heartless purple-gray tinge hung in the air, and worse yet, it smelled moist and dank like a wet stray puppy. The air even felt heavy, like someone, an evil genius perhaps, had turned up gravity.

Despite the ominous sky, Ted's spirits remained undampened. He held his square chin high, a smile on his seldom expressed lips. His eyes, usually narrow and distantly cold, were sparkling with life and wide open. Never had he been this happy. He looked at Kate, at her goldenrod hair cascaded around her shoulders, and grinned even wider. Stopping at the white Thunderbird, he leaned on the roof.

Kate gazed at Ted, dumbfounded by his actions. "What's up Ted?" she queried.

"I need the keys," he replied, reducing the size but not the intention of his smile.

Kate fished in her pockets, producing a silver key ring. She tossed the ring over the hood of the car. Ted snatched it from the darkening air with a scooping swipe. He unlocked the door, then slid into the driver's seat, activating the power locks with a quick flick of his index finger. Kate loaded herself into the interior of the Ford, and, with a symphony of snapping seatbelts, they headed for the Northtown Mall a few blocks away.

Ted entered at the northern end of the lot, not because Kate was parked there but because he could not cross the divided highway at the southern entrance. Weaving his way through the parking lot, Ted drove slowly toward the area he parked in when he first arrived three hours ago. "Over there," Kate mumbled, pointing to a tan Oldsmobile parked beneath a tall lamp. Ted pulled into the unoccupied parking stall to the immediate left of the sedan, gently applying the brakes. Bringing the Thunderbird to a halt, Ted pushed the lever into the park position.

Kate climbed out of the automobile, black handbag on her shoulder, keys in dainty hand. Ted also climbed from the sports coupe. He placed his right foot on the running board, his left foot on the blacktop. His right forearm and hand rested on the white roof. Standing in that position, he watched Kate unlock her driver's side door. She tossed the black purse into the passenger seat, then peered over the ceiling of the Thunderbird at Ted.

"Thanks for everything."

"No problem," he replied.

"I'll see you later." She ducked into the car, scooting into the driver's seat and pulling her protective harness taut across her chest.

"See ya." Ted raised his right hand. He let the limb drop to rest on the roof of the Ford as Kate pulled shut the door of her Oldsmobile.

Kate backed out of the parking stall, then shifted the Oldsmobile into drive. She followed the path out of the parking lot, turning right onto Wellesley. Ted followed her progress, standing rigidly in place. He watched Kate reach the intersection, turning right again through a green light. Once on Division, she opened the throttle.

Ted followed her with his eyes until she finally slipped from sight, heading north on Division into the twilight. Ted lowered his suddenly fatigued body into the Thunderbird, wriggling into a comfortable position. Grabbing a compact disc, he pushed the item into the player. With a shaky right index finger, he tapped a button on the car stereo until a display indicated the number of the track he wanted. The music filled the cabin, a slow song by a female singer with a strong voice. As she sang, a cascade of tears began to slide down Ted's cheeks. Rubbing his swollen eyes, Ted sat in the idling Thunderbird and sobbed.

12

"I hadn't cried that hard since Granpa died. Nothing had been that important to me, that real. Even though it only lasted a few minutes, I still feel sad about not having her and would like to cry some more.

Then again, I also am happy that I got my opportunity. That's why I was so excited when I got back here tonight. I mean, I won Ratscrew for the first time ever! I have to believe that this can only be a beginning. We will have more times to share, more adventures to experience together. It has to happen. Something so right is destined to survive."

Annie finished the sentence, her raspy voice trailing off. She pressed her right thumb and index finger lightly into her tear ducts, holding up her wireframe glasses with her left hand. Wiping her flushed cheeks of moisture with her right fist, she closed the beaten cover of the green spiral notebook and placed it on her lap. She adjusted her glasses on her face, then sobbed quietly, seated on the floral print couch.

Rubbing her eyes, she read the clock, ticking slowly on the far wall. *Oh my Gosh!* she thought, *I've wasted an hour!* Frantic, Annie scooped up the notebook and scrambled into the kitchen, dodging through a maze of cardboard boxes. Dropping the notebook on the kitchen counter, just left of the sink, she tore open a nearby cabinet. Annie pulled a knife from the deep drawer, using the blade to carve into a strip of duct tape that sealed a cardboard box marked "Dishes" in black Magic Marker. Annie discarded the knife nonchalantly, letting it bounce off the counter and rest against the side of the box. She spread open the lid of the box, then pulled the plates from their cardboard sarcophagus. Throwing open a cupboard door, she strained to push the stack onto an upper shelf. She rose to her toes, reaching as high as her five-foot-one frame would allow. The plates rattled together as they clawed their way onto the ledge. Annie backed away and pulled down the waist of her purple sweatshirt, which had crept up to expose her navel and midriff. Pleased with her accomplishment, she slapped the prefabricated cabinet door, letting it fall shut with a hollow clap of wood on wood. Brushing her sweaty brow, she glanced again at the closed green notebook.

A flood of memories overflowed her mind, saturating her thoughts with the vivid contents of the spiral notebook. Annie breathed deeply, letting thoughts of chance meetings in faraway towns and images of country swing dancing pervade her subconscious. She grinned as she remembered the tale of the crazy party. She basked in the warmth of the story of the date, the beautiful evening shared between two great friends. After reflecting on the incredible charm of the entire volume of work, the happiness in her heart faded away.

Annie's thoughts turned to the man that had written the journal. She imagined the build of Ted. Fluttering shut her eyes, she pictured Ted's tall, lanky frame, two long, skinny arms and two legs lacking muscle definition. She thought of his strong, square jaw, his parted dusty brown hair, his hands sweeping through the haircut. The picture continued to clear; she envisioned his pouting lips, then watched the pair curl into a smile as she mentioned the name of his love in her mind. His dark eyes opened, exposing a brilliant hazel-blue iris that sparkled at the thought of his love. The shadows over his murky image disappeared, and the picture cleared. Annie kept her eyes tightly shut, fighting to hold on to the thought of a gentleman any woman, her included, would want in their lives.

Annie opened her eyes, focusing once more on the green journal. "I've gotta keep this," she muttered softly, barely able to audibly choke out the words. Her eyes itched, beginning to fill with more salty tears. She picked up the journal, clutching it tightly to her chest. Taking a deep breath, she turned on her toe to leave the kitchen.

"Jesus!" she exclaimed, tensing her back and legs at the sight of a figure leaning against the corridor wall. She caught her breath, trying to get her heart rate to slow. "Barry! You scared the heck outta me!"

"Sorry, Annie dear," he heckled. "Didn't mean to."

"It's okay. How long have you been standing there?"

"A couple of seconds." Barry flashed a glance around the kitchen, darting his emerald eyes over full boxes and empty pantries. "You not get much done?"

"No. I didn't." Annie looked away, ashamed.

Barry took a step forward, studying her bloodshot, moistly glistening eyes and flushed cheeks. "You okay? You been crying?"

"Yes, and yes." She dabbed at her eyes, wicking away moisture from the ducts with her right thumb and forefinger. She hugged the notebook close to her sternum, placing her right hand over her left on the journal's ravaged cover.

Barry fixed his gaze on the spiral packet of paper sheets. "Hey, what's that?"

"It's a notebook I found," Annie replied, drumming her fingers on the cover. "It was in one of the drawers in the kitchen." She clutched her find even tighter.

"Is that what made you cry?" Barry reached out his right hand, resting the palm lightly on Annie's left shoulder.

Annie gulped. Her eyes glistened, loaded heavily with a payload of tears. "Uh huh," she nodded, a drop of water breaking free from the corner of her swollen left eye as she blinked.

"So, if you read it…what's it about?"

Annie raised her eyes, meeting with Barry's concerned, pained gaze. Tears began to tumble recklessly down her reddened cheeks, escaping with each flutter of her eyelids. She gulped a gasp of air, sighed deeply, and replied to Barry's question.

"It's about me."

Barry tried to grab her, to hug her, but she backed away. Tucking the notebook under her left arm, Annie twisted the door knob nearest the counter. The door opened, exposing the balcony that attached to the second-story apartment. Sobbing breathlessly, Annie stepped out onto the weathertreated platform and leaned against a wooden railing. She placed both forearms on the journal's battered cover, then buried her tear ravaged face in her crossed arms. Weeping gently, Kathleen Anne Whipple looked up from her downward gaze, squinting with swollen eyelids into a bright, happy sun.

About the Author

Chad Taylor is a graduate of Eastern Washington University in Cheney, Washington. This is his first novel.

Printed in the United States
32739LVS00003B/866